MY BEAUTIFUL POISON

T.L. SMITH

MY
BEAUTIFUL
POISON

CHAPTER
1

Rylee

My lip is bleeding. It tastes—I lick it again—sweet. I like the taste. Is that weird? I had heard it's meant to have a metallic taste. But mine, well, it's sweet. Maybe it's the only thing about me that is sweet.

My fingers touch the edges of my lips. The bleeding is slowing, but the throbbing intensifies.

"Fuck, Rylee, really?"

My hand drops away from my busted lip as I glance up at him.

He's shaking his head, his blond hair barely moving with all the product he uses. "See what you made me do? Fuck!" He swipes his face with his hand and stares at me with emotionless eyes.

How could I have been so blind to those eyes for so long?

"You should leave..." I somehow manage to whisper then lick my lips—I can still taste the sweetness of my blood.

He tries to touch me again, but I step back dramatically.

"Leave, Anderson," I say with more force.

He shakes his head and scrubs his face again.

Really? How many times does he plan to do that? Doesn't he know by touching his face he's spreading germs?

"Rylee, come on..."

Sidestepping him, I open my bedroom door. "You better leave before I scream." I blink a few times and then glare. "If you don't, I'll kick you where I *know* the sun doesn't shine."

Anger rolls between his brows while his hands tighten into fists. "You need to watch your mouth," he grates out through gritted teeth, his voice hard and unrelenting.

"Ha," I bark out, shaking my head. "Last strike." I point to my face and then the door. "Now, *leave* and *don't* come back."

Anderson takes a step in my direction then leans down so his face is close to mine. "They would never believe you over me. And even if they did, they won't care. All they want is for you to marry me." He smirks and steps toward the door. He lifts his hand, and I hold my flinch in as he grips the door handle. "I'll see you tomorrow, Rylee."

I watch him step out the door and down my parents' stairs, saying goodbye to them as he leaves.

I hate him.

What I ever saw in him, I'll never know.

It's hard, but I need to get out of this house. My parents expect and want so much from me. Sometimes, I wish I had followed my sister, Rhianna, when she escaped the family business. To be honest, I don't know why I didn't leave with her. Perhaps it wasn't the right time, but now regret chips away at my heart every single day. Every single minute. How do you combat what you want with what is right for you?

With a hard push, I close the door and then slide down its surface. My hands cover my face as I draw my knees up under my chin.

I've been dating Anderson since high school. He was the popular football player, and I was the good little rich girl.

Our parents couldn't be more pleased with

our relationship. Fuck, they're already planning our wedding and I'm only twenty-three.

I don't want to get married this young, and especially not to *him.*

Anderson has his good days, but he has far too many bad ones. And let's be quite serious here, I don't want any days with him.

I hear footsteps approach my door, and I know who it is straight away.

"Ry, tell me you're okay?" my little brother whispers, his concern floating to me through the closed door.

"I'm fine, Beckham. I'll see you in the morning," I tell him with the strongest voice I can muster.

He waits.

He always does.

He's the only one who understands what Anderson is like, and he hates him for it. But, more importantly, he detests that I won't leave him, and he can't grasp the concept of why I stay. It makes him crazy angry, but I can't seem to muster the energy to do what I know is right.

It's the pressure.

The pressure from my family is simply too much.

My father takes care of the accounts of some

of the wealthiest people in Australia, and that extends to the rest of the world. I'm his only child who's willing to, or even interested in, taking over the family business. I work with Father now, understanding the basics, as I have finally finished my degree in accounting. And soon, I will run it all. Which makes me happy. I like what I do—numbers and money makes me happy. I like to organize and find the number's rightful place then fix any problems that arise in handling the accounts.

Plus, I'm good at it.

Really good.

My sister is what you'd call a free spirit. She's never done well listening to rules and prefers to travel and live her life the way she wants—carefree and easy-going. My brother is a football star. Even at his young age of sixteen, we all know he's going places.

So that leaves me, Rylee Harley, twin sister to Rhianna Harley and older sister to Beckham, to fill the spot that's left open. Our parents want to retire, live a life of luxury, which my father deserves. He is one of the hardest workers I know. Dedicated. Loyal. Committed.

I do adore them both, no matter what others think.

Even if my mother is overbearing, she's still my mother.

It's all about the pressure.

The pressure to be perfect.

And this crushes my spirit and steals pieces of me every day.

Anderson is right at the top of the list of pressure.

I did love him, once.

He's handsome, all the women want him, and I can't blame them. Anderson comes from money, is athletic, and could charm the panties right off you. Which was what he did to me.

I didn't win any popularity contests in school like my sister. I kept my head down and was studious.

Until Anderson.

Then everyone knew who I was.

I was no longer Rhianna's quiet twin sister. I was Rylee, Anderson's girlfriend, and I have been for way too long.

My phone beeps, and I know immediately who it is. My head swings in that direction and I watch as it lights up, then goes dark. In exactly one minute, it'll do it again. I watch, waiting. And like clockwork, it does just that. Lights up again.

Now, he's apologizing.

And I will *not* read his texts.

I don't want to read them.

Anderson set up my phone to show him when I read his messages, so he'll know I haven't. It's just another way for him to control me.

And another way I let him.

Today wasn't the first time he's hit my face. He's usually careful not to leave a mark like he's done today, though. I lick my lip and still taste the blood lingering there.

I never thought I would be one of *those* girls, but here I am.

Staring at my phone from across the room, I and wishing it would disappear, I can't stand to think about his fake apologies that lay on it.

Taking a deep breath, I shake my head and stand. Reaching for my phone, I don't open the messages like he wants me to. Instead, I walk it to my bathroom and fill the bathtub. I watch as the water stills when I turn the faucet off and then I smile as the phone slips from my hand and drops into the crystal-clear water.

Tomorrow is the day I start living for me.

Or so I keep telling myself.

CHAPTER
2

My fingers tap on the table that my hands are cuffed to, and my leg bounces, unable to move or go anywhere unless I figure out a way to cut my fucking hands off. I wait for him to arrive—the only person left who has an ounce of faith in me, apart from my baby sister.

Why? Well, I'm still trying to work that out.

The loud noise doesn't make me jump anymore as they open the doors behind me. His expensive shoes come into view, and I glance up to Noah, who offers me a smile as he takes a seat across from me. His eyes drop to my chained hands then he glances over to the guard.

"Undo his hands," he snaps. "Now."

The guard does as he asks, and my wrists are freed.

Noah flips through his paperwork and slides something across the table to me.

"This is your grandmother's will." I scrunch my face as I scan the document. "She left you the house," Noah states.

My grandmother died over four years ago. Why am I only now hearing about this? "From the look on your face, it seems your last lawyer conveniently forgot to disclose any of this to you."

He guessed right.

"My grandmother hated me," I tell him. She was always telling me to get my act together and do something with my life, or I would turn out like my deadbeat mother.

Perhaps she was right.

"Yeah, well... it seems she loved you, regardless."

"Paige?" I ask.

My little sister has a good father. He knew our mother was scum and took her away early, leaving me to clean up the mess my mother created. And my father? Well, I don't even know who he is and couldn't care less, either.

"She's doing well. Your grandmother left her a car. Which I'm sure Paige has told you in her letters."

Paige is almost sixteen, and in her letters, she's told me how excited she is to start driving. She's asked to visit me, but that's not an option. This isn't somewhere she should frequent. Not ever.

"I have some other news for you, August." Noah closes the folder in front of him and leans back in his chair. His eyes flick to the guard, then back to me. "You'll be released tomorrow. The judge approved your appeal."

His words don't register.

I don't understand them.

I simply stare at him, as if he's grown a second head.

Because that would never happen. I'm only six years into a long sentence and not once has any of my appeals even been heard.

Yet, here's Noah, a man I hardly know, who has become my one and only friend, telling me I am finally going to be free.

I rub the stubble on my jaw and eye him. "You're lying."

"Do I seem like a man who lies, August?"

No. Noah has never lied to me. No matter how hard the truth may have been, he has always given it to me straight. "I had a cleaner go around to your grandmother's today, seeing as no one has been living there for all this time."

I can't even come up with the words to thank him. So, all I do is nod my head.

"I'll be back tomorrow to pick you up." Noah stands, gathering his things. He strolls to the door, but I stay where I am, still in shock. "August…" he says my name, and I check over my shoulder, "… don't fuck this up. They'll be eager to throw you straight back in here the first chance they get."

It's more than obvious, and I know they'll be looking for me to fuck up. The same way they easily threw me in here. Trash is what they said when they caught and tossed me into the back of the cop car.

"Noah," I say. "I owe you one."

"You owe me nothing," he says, then continues on his way out the door.

I grip my hair.

Fuck.

Free.

I never thought this day would come.

Destined to end up in here, I was nothing more than a street thug. My mother always said so. So when it finally happened, I wasn't all that surprised.

But getting out now, because of a man I hardly know who chose to fight for me?

It's a fucking miracle.

CHAPTER
3

It's been two days, and I have managed to avoid Anderson. Not once have I seen nor heard from him. It helps that my phone is still lying at the bottom of my bathtub, never to work again.

Rhianna steps into my office, dressed in her work outfit, which consists of shorts and a shirt, and the apron she usually wears is wrapped around her small waist. Her long, dark hair is tied up on her head while mine is in a half-up, half-down ponytail. Her dark, almost black eyes, that mirror mine, stare at me.

Identical. In almost every way, physically.

Twins. With two uniquely different personalities.

Best friends. For all the right reasons.

My ride-or-die.

"Noah is celebrating tonight. I wanted to see if you would come." My eyes go to the pile of paperwork in front of me. I use it as an excuse. Often. Especially to Anderson.

"I..." Rhianna shakes her head before I can even finish getting my first word out.

"Don't forget I know you. Like, *really* know you. So don't even try to use that shit in front of you as an excuse," Rhianna says, her hands lifting and pulling her hair out of its bun as she watches me. "All you have time for now is Anderson and work. News flash..." she waves her hands around dramatically, "... I am way more important than both."

I smirk at her words. Because they're true. Oh so true.

"I can dress you," she offers with a smile.

I shake my head. "It's fine. I'll head home soon and get changed."

"I've been trying to call you. Why is your phone switched off?"

"I drowned it," I reply with a smirk.

Her eyes go wide. "Should I ask?"

I shrug my shoulders. "Probably not. I have ordered a new one and should get it tomorrow. I'll send you the number." She stands, putting her bag over her shoulder and then across her body. "How's Noah?" I ask. It's her first real relationship. He's older than us and an incredibly successful businessman.

A smile touches her lips at the mention of his name. "He's good. Really good. I plan to marry that man."

"I'm glad he makes you happy."

She goes still at my words, ambles around my desk, and leans down. "You need to find someone who makes you happy, too. Clearly, Anderson is *not* that man."

He isn't, and I am well aware of that fact.

"I'm working on it," I reply truthfully. And I am. All that's been running through my head is how I plan to break it off with Anderson officially. Only it's not just him I have to tell, it's my parents too. They have already planned our massive wedding, and we aren't even engaged.

"If you do it and need me to be the insolent child to take the heat off of you, I got ya." She winks.

I laugh because I know she's telling the truth. She has no problem with disappointing our parents, especially our mother. Where, for some reason, it physically makes me ill to do so.

"Seven?" I ask.

She kisses my cheek before she walks out of my office, telling me, "Yes," as she leaves.

Anderson's car was in my driveway when I pulled in, so I reversed straight back out and drove to Rhianna's, knowing she wasn't going to be home. Stepping straight into her closet, I retrieve an outfit and get ready. Luckily for me, we're the exact same size, but we don't dress the same. I do have a few pieces of clothing hanging in her closet for emergencies, and tonight definitely qualifies as an emergency. However, I don't choose one of my dresses. Instead, I go for something different.

I leave my hair the way it is and pick one of Rhianna's black dresses that stops just above my knee. I add some lip gloss and call an Uber, leaving my car at my sister's house.

Noah's having the event at a local restaurant, so I chose low heels for the occasion. I really have no idea what we're celebrating. I agreed because she wanted me there. And if I need her, she's always there for me.

When I arrive at the restaurant, instantly I know I'm overdressed. Way overdressed. Not one of the women is wearing a dress. They're all in lunch attire, even though it's evening. Some are wearing jeans, some skirts, but nothing fancy. Striding in, I spot my sister straight away, her arm around Noah as he talks to someone and she's hanging on his every word. Noah spots me and waves me over, making Rhianna glance up. She removes herself from him and smiles.

"You didn't go home?" she asks, noticing her dress.

"No," I reply, causing both of them to scan my body. "Good to see you again, Noah."

"Always a pleasure, Rylee. Thanks for coming. Is Anderson with you tonight?"

"No."

"There's an open bar. Help yourself. Your sister has been," he jokes, making Rhianna wiggle her eyebrows.

"You want to get drunk and go skinny dipping?" she asks.

Noah's watching Rhianna with eager eyes. He literally only has eyes for her, and it makes me so happy for her.

"I'm going to get a drink," I respond, not answering that question. If you give her an inch, she will take a mile and then run with it.

"Or ten," Rhianna calls to my back, which makes me chuckle.

When I step up to the bar, I order a gin and tonic with lime.

"Didn't take you for the drinking type," a dark

voice says right next to me. My eyes find that voice, and the first thing I see is tanned hands followed by strong forearms with prominent veins.

Arm porn.

Vein porn.

When I manage to move my eyes away from those sexy arms, I blink, once, twice, three times. I can't believe what I'm seeing.

I haven't seen him since high school, and even then, he was someone you never got too close to. And here I am, standing next to him as he nurses a drink in his hand.

"It's water, if you must know," he says as I glance at his face after staring at his glass for a few moments.

August has been in prison for over six years, and I know his sentence was for much longer than that.

How is he standing here next to me? I have no idea.

"August," I say, to which he nods then looks away, bringing the glass to his lips and taking a sip. I watch as he swallows, then the glass is placed on the countertop again.

"Rich girl remembers." His voice is a deep timbre, his hair the color of mahogany, deep and rich, with only subtle hues of light—nothing like Anderson's. In school, August was two years above me in grades, but *everyone* knew who he was. He was the bad boy that every girl wanted despite being scared of him.

And believe me, every girl with eyes wanted him.

August Trouble had an air of mystery about himself. No one ever seriously knew him, and the few girls who claimed they did, talked about him as if he were some sort of god.

He hasn't changed much. He still has that hard air about him. Except now, he has a scar above his lip, his face is sharper, the angles more prominent, and his hair is shorter than the undercut he had in school. He's bigger—a *lot* bigger.

"Do you even know my name?" I ask.

Rich girl. That's definitely not my name.

His eyes, green as the forest, shine back at me.

"Rich girl," is all he says, then taps his fingertips on the bar.

"That is *not* my name," I declare, turning my nose up at him.

August bites his bottom lip, his scar becoming more prominent as he does, and he turns to check me over with those eyes. The black dress suddenly feels all sorts of wrong on my body.

"Rhianna," he says in a fast breath.

I try to not deflate. I mean, if you don't know us, it's hard to tell us apart. And this man hasn't seen either of us in six years, so there's no way he could tell us apart.

Plus, we were nothing to him in school.

He was a king.

I was nothing but a girl who went to school every day, trying to hide in the shadows.

"I better be going." I pick up my drink and wander back to my sister, not looking back over my shoulder at the man with great arms and who thinks I am my sister. As soon as I reach her, her hand grabs mine, and she pulls me so we're standing next to each other.

"I saw you chatting to August," she whispers while her other hand stays in Noah's. "I forgot to tell you this party… it's for him. Noah got him out."

Now it all makes sense.

"He's an asshole." I lift my drink and check over my shoulder. He's exactly where I left him, staring at his drink as people mingle all around him.

Rhianna bumps me, and I turn to her. "You had a crush on him all through school. If you wanted to…" She glances back at him. "I mean… I bet he hasn't had sex in a long time." Her eyebrows wiggle at her suggestion.

"No. Just no."

"I bet Anderson hasn't ever made you come," she finishes.

"Anderson," a voice says from behind me.

Spinning around, I see August now standing there.

"August, you remember my sister," Rhianna says.

"Of course, Rylee." He winks at me, and I narrow my eyes at him.

The damn asshole. He knew my name all along and decided to upset me by using my sister's name. Well, two can play that game.

"She had a major crush on you during school," my sister tells him.

Oh, god. My cheeks go red at her words, and thankfully, before either of us can say anything, Noah walks over and taps August on the shoulder.

"You ready?" he asks.

August nods.

Rhianna leans in and kisses my cheek. "We're going. You going back to mine?"

"Yeah, don't think I want to head home just yet," I tell her. I can feel August's eyes on me as I speak, but I choose not to glance his way.

"Okay. I was going to stay at Noah's, but I can come with you if you need me to."

I hold up my hand. "No, don't be silly. I can crash at yours."

"I love you," she says.

Noah waves as they head off. August stepping off first, not saying a word to me as he leaves.

And that's probably for the best.

CHAPTER
4

August

The house is empty and lonely. Noah picked me up from the prison and drove me out to my new home. Not hearing voices yelling from another cell, which somehow became something I had expected to hear, made my first night here difficult, to say the least. I hardly slept, and when I couldn't, I went out to the yard to tackle that. It's quite clear no one has been here for what seems like forever. I'm glad Noah managed to get the house cleaned. If the yard is anything to go by, I would've hated to have seen it before it was tidied and scrubbed. And that's saying something considering where I have spent the last six years. But then again, anything is better than there.

And I mean anything.

By the third day post-prison, the yard is looking better. It's starting to resemble something like a normal house again.

"August." I hear Paige's voice before I see her. Turning around, my little sister jumps into my arms and wraps hers tight around me.

It's the first time I have been hugged in a long time.

A very long time.

My hands hang at my sides because I don't know what to do. Hugging is so damn foreign to me.

I see her father standing next to his car, not taking his eyes off of her for one second as she releases me. I ruffle her long hair as she pulls back.

"You look good, kid. So big." She was a pipsqueak when I went away all those years ago, and the letters here and there occasionally containing a picture are nothing compared to what she's like in person.

"I'm almost an adult, you know."

My lips turn up in the corners at her words. "I've missed you."

She leans back in and wraps her arms around me again.

"I've missed you more." We stay like that for a little while until her father calls her name. "I told him he was either taking me, or I would find my own way to see you."

"I would've come and seen you, squeak." She's my top priority of absolutes, but I needed to get my head on straight first.

"August." Glenn, her father, walks across the yard and nods his head in my direction. "It's good to see you."

"Thanks for bringing her around."

Glenn glances past me to the house. "You've done a lot in a few days. This place was starting to look haunted," he says, then his eyes travel back to mine.

My sister grins.

"You seen your mother?" He cut all contact with the woman when he took Paige from her care. I hated him for it at the time, but now I am glad he did. I would hate to see Paige broken the way I am. Her soul is too kind for that to happen to her.

"No."

Glenn nods, happy with that answer.

"Time to go, Paige. Say goodbye to your brother."

"I want to stay. I can help, August. Please, let me help."

"That's not a good idea. We have plans," Glenn says.

"It's fine, squeak. Another time, I'm sure."

Glenn grins. "Yes, another time."

Paige wraps her arms around my waist again before she pulls back, and I watch as they both depart, leaving me alone once again.

I'm used to solitude, so it makes no difference.

The stares and the whispers are what I expected. But dealing with it isn't something I was mentally prepared for. Before I was locked away, I got the same reactions, but not to this extent. Now everyone knows who I am, so when I walk into the grocery store to buy some food for the house, women hold their purses a little tighter, and the cashier flinches when he sees me.

I head straight to the back to pick up the staples—bread, milk, and snacks. Basically, just enough so I don't have to come back here anytime soon.

"You need to leave," a voice pipes up from behind me.

When I turn, I see a rent-a-cop dressed in blue, holding onto his utility belt like Batman as he stares at me. He's old, and in one movement, I could have him on the floor. Instead, I bite my tongue and stroll past him, going straight to the cashier with the groceries I have in hand.

He follows me, his boots clicking behind me.

The cashier glances at the asshole rent-a-cop before looking directly at me.

"Leave," the fake cop, or should I say security guard, barks behind me again.

"I need to purchase this, then I'll leave," I reply, biting my cheek a little too hard, so much so I taste the metallic tang of blood. It's the only thing stopping me from turning around and showing him who I really am.

But I'm changing.

I have to.

The old me was dangerous and unpredictable. I need to be a better me. Otherwise, I'll end up where I just left.

"You aren't welcome here," he snarls.

I give the cashier a grin, ignoring the rent-a-cop. "Ring me up, so I can leave," I tell him.

He's young, and his eyes shift behind me again, where I know the rent-a-cop is standing.

"No, leave," the young guy says.

Fuck! I clutch my wallet in my hand and think how easy it would be to simply knock them both the fuck out. I could walk out with the stuff I want and not care, but I want to be better than that. Better than these two knuckleheads.

However, I won't because that's exactly what they want. And one wrong move will lead me back to the one place I just escaped from.

And I do *not* want to go back.

Stepping back, I turn and march out. As soon as I step out the door, my stomach growls. I ordered takeout last night, and I am fucking starving now, but I can't keep wasting my money on takeout. At least not until I find a job.

"Here." I turn to see a dark-haired beauty standing in front of me, sunglasses covering her face as she holds a paper bag out to me. "Take it, August. Before my hand falls off."

I take the bag and check inside. It's full of everything I was trying to buy. As I look back up, Rylee is staring at me through her glasses. Then she turns and strolls away. I watch as she hotfoots it to her expensive car. And just before she gets in, I call out to her, "Rich girl."

She turns back. "Yes?" Her nose is scrunched up at my choice of name for her.

"I'm not your fucking charity case," I spit out.

Rylee shakes her head before she slides in her car and drives off. A part of me wants to throw the shit at her car, but I know better. I need food. And despite her being a rich girl, she is fucking hot and generous, even though I don't want to admit that right now.

"You've done heaps," Noah says the next day as he steps inside. He checks around, his hands by his sides, exuding so much confidence it's almost enough to make me physically ill.

"Yep," Is all I reply.

Noah walks to the back door and views the yard, which I have torn to pieces and flattened. Not even a bush is standing where it used to be.

"How are you going with getting supplies?" he asks. "I heard about the supermarket."

"Of course you did. She can't keep her mouth shut."

"Who?" Noah asks.

"Rylee."

"What does Rylee have to do with the supermarket?" he asks with an appearance of confusion crossing his face.

"She was there. It wasn't her that told you?"

"No, one of my clients saw it all and let me know."

Well, fuck. Rich girl kept her mouth shut. I'll be damned.

"What do you plan to do for work? Your grandmother left you some money, but there's not a lot."

"I haven't gotten that far. Though, I guess, it's something I should look into." Except for the fact that I've never worked a real job in my life.

"Do you want me to get you some work?"

I scrub my hand down my face and sit at the dining room table as he turns and stares.

"No."

"August, this will only work if you go back to living a normal life."

I chuckle.

What *is* a *normal* life? Even before prison, my life was anything but normal. My mother was the town whore, doing whatever she could for her next drink, even my damn friends. Disgusting.

Normal life? Yeah, I don't know what that is.

"You can be whoever you want to be, August. If you look at it that way, I'll do whatever I can to assist you."

My knuckles rap on the table. "Why?" I ask. He's done everything for free, and he's one of the best lawyers in the city. His reputation as the next big thing is renowned, and yet, here he is, helping me.

"I don't know if I told you this, but I was married before."

I shake my head because I had no idea. Though we don't share many personal things.

"She was a great woman. She told me I shouldn't do everything for the greedy, that I should remember where I came from. Remember my roots." He stares at me. "I remember, August. And believe it or not, we have a very similar backstory. My mother was someone you wouldn't wish on your worst nightmare, and my father was never in the picture."

"And look at you now," I say to him, surprised by his words.

"And look at you. You're free. Now, make the most of it," he says before he heads out the same way he came in, leaving me to ponder his words of wisdom.

CHAPTER
5

Rylee

"Rylee."

Fuck.

Fuck.

I didn't see his car out the front. *How did I miss that?*

"We need to talk."

Ha, no stinking way.

"Rylee, dear, Anderson has been waiting for hours to see you. Seems he keeps missing you."

My mother's eyes narrow on me as if she knows I've been avoiding him. Hell, she probably does.

"Yes, let's talk," Anderson says and begins the journey up the stairs to my bedroom. I place my bag down on the floor as I watch him disappear.

"What are you waiting for, Rylee?" my mother asks as I stay where I am.

Turning to her, I see so much of me in my mother. The same color hair and bone structure. But it's the eyes that stare back at me that aren't mine. Hers are hard and demanding. She has expectations. I live in *her* reality.

What I should do is move out, leave this house. It's not as if I'm not old enough or don't earn enough money to set myself up. It's been easier living here while studying and working, but now I don't have any reason to stay.

I think it's way past time, though.

"I'm going to move out," I tell her. Her brows shoot up in surprise. "I'm going to start searching for a place tomorrow."

"What about your brother? He enjoys having you here."

"He can visit whenever he wants. He knows that."

"You'll end up just like your sister," she warns.

"And there is nothing wrong with that. Rhianna is with a man who makes her happy. She has traveled the world and loves what she does right now, even if it's not what you want." My head turns back to the stairs.

My mother isn't a bad person, simply demanding, and I've come to know how to work her better than either of my siblings.

"I have a ring picked out," my mother chimes when I don't give her my attention.

"Throw it away," I say, as I begin the climb up the stairs, my hand gripping the banister, my knuckles turning white with the realization I'll be in the same room with *him* by myself, and we all know that never turns out well—*for me.*

Anderson is standing at my door, leaning against it as he watches me walk past him. His eyes roam over me from top to bottom before he whispers, "I missed you."

I shudder.

I haven't missed him at all.

Not even in the slightest.

"You haven't been answering your phone."

"I drowned it." I smirk as I tell him.

He laughs as if it's some sort of joke.

"I'll get you a new one." Anderson reaches out and pulls me to him by my waist. I go because fighting him isn't worth the hassle right now. "I've missed you," he says again as he leans down and kisses my neck.

My hands remain by my sides, not lifting or touching him in any way, even if he doesn't seem to notice or care.

"We need to talk."

"Yes, later," he says, his mouth leaving sloppy kisses all over mine. I attempt to pull away, but he keeps me close, his hands grasping hard, causing bruises, I'm sure. "I need you."

"Not now, Anderson. I want to talk."

"Later," he says in a deeper, more stern voice.

I try to push away, but he doesn't let me. "Anderson... Let. Me. Go."

"No. You need to be reminded of how suited we are for each other."

"No, I do not." I pull back.

He stares at me. "You do. You love me." He goes for my lips, and his mouth comes down hard on them. Anderson is a shit kisser—too hard and too sloppy. I don't give him access, but that doesn't stop him from taking what he wants as he tries to keep kissing me.

Managing to pull out of his embrace, I escape his hands and separate us.

"You need to leave." He steps toward me, but I hold up my hand. "*Leave*," I say in a voice I didn't know I was capable of.

Anderson's eyes lock on mine. It's then he sees me. Sees I don't want him. And when he does, a look passes across his face that truly makes me scared.

"You are *mine*, Rylee."

"I am not. I am *mine*, Anderson. No one owns me."

He laughs. "Bullshit! Everyone owns you. Your parents. Me. Fuck, who else does?"

"I'm my own person, and I don't want you here anymore."

"You don't get to decide that, Rylee. You'll be my wife soon," he says through gritted teeth with a touch of smugness in his voice.

"I *won't* marry you," I tell him with as much force as I can muster. "I want you to leave and never come back."

I watch as his top lip quirks up, then back down.

"You seem to be delusional right now." He

takes a breath. "I'll give you a week to get your head right. That's all I'm giving you, Rylee. Then I *will* be taking what's mine." Anderson reaches for me again, and I manage to step back so his hands don't touch me. He glares at me with hard, uncaring eyes that hold no emotion. He doesn't care about me. I'm simply a means to an end for him. A trophy, and I won't have it. I won't allow him to come near me again.

"Just leave, Anderson. I don't know how many more times I have to say it."

His teeth grind at my words, but he turns and shifts through the doorway quickly, slamming it so hard the adjoining walls rattle.

Finally pulling my bag down and off my shoulder, the door opens again, but this time, my mother is standing there.

"What was that about?" She glances at my bag, which is on the floor, and steps in, picking it up and placing it on the bed. "Are you two fighting?" she asks while checking around the room.

"I won't marry him. Hell, I don't even want to see him again."

She pauses and fixes her attention on me. "You simply need sleep," she says and turns toward the door.

"Why do you want me to marry him so

badly?"

"Because you've been with him forever, and he adores you. He can support you in any way you wish."

"I can support myself, Mother," I say back to her. "And I may have been with him since high school, but now I've grown up, I want better for myself. He's cheated on me. You want me to be with someone who doesn't respect me?"

"You think you can do better than Anderson? He comes from the best family in the country. Everyone knows who they are."

"I *know* I can do better. *Anyone* is better than Anderson," I retort back with more venom than I meant to. It's not her fault. She simply doesn't know what an awful human he is.

"His mother loves you, and she doesn't like anyone," she says. "That right there tells me you are perfect for each other."

"You're delusional." I shake my head and walk to the door, standing there holding it open. "I need some rest. I have work tomorrow."

She rushes past me as she heads out the door. "Just think about what you're doing. Your life with Anderson could be perfect."

I scoff at her and shut the door behind her

with perhaps a little more enthusiasm than I should have as it slams shut.

No. My life with *that man* would be a nightmare.

Of that, I am one hundred percent certain.

Our city is large, but the town we live in is small. It seems everyone knows everything about everyone. People gossip. The rich mingle and tell each other everything, then they tell the others, and it never stops. It's like a game of telephone, gossip, slandering each other—it's horrible to witness most of the time.

So when August's name pops up, I lean in closer to listen as I sit across from my sister at a local café the next afternoon.

"I mean, I know he's bad. But have you seen him? I would like to use and abuse that body, that's for sure." I roll my eyes at the girl's words and Rhianna giggles.

"You've been avoiding going home most of the week," Rhianna says, lifting her milkshake and bringing it to her lips. "I mean... you know you're always welcome in my home, but don't you think it's time we find you your own place?"

"I was planning on doing exactly that."

Her eyebrows shoot up in surprise. "You

plan to leave the confines of our parents' house?"

I nod.

"Please tell me it's not with that loser," she says with an eye roll.

"No. I'm leaving him." I watch as Rhianna's eyes go wide.

"Have you told him that?"

I tuck my hair behind my ear and glance down to my coffee that's going cold. "I've been trying, but he really isn't taking the hint even though I'm using a sledgehammer to deliver it."

"Want me to pretend to be you? I'm sure I can *make* him take the hint."

She used to swap with me in school when I couldn't cope with things, and she could.

Problem with this little scenario is that Anderson can tell us apart.

"No, I have to do it."

"Good, he's a dick anyway."

"That he is," I agree.

"Tomorrow then. Tomorrow, we'll search for a house for you."

I give her a simple nod in agreement.

The girls next to us start talking again about August. I stay quiet but listen intently.

"He's the talk of the town," Rhianna says. "They're either scared of him or want him."

"I saw him," I tell her.

"Where?"

"At the supermarket. He was trying to buy food, but they wouldn't serve him." Her eyes go wide. "I bought it for him, but he wasn't impressed."

"You bought food for him?"

"Yes, I'm not a bitch, Rhi," I reply, shaking my head.

She holds up her hands. "Never said you were, but I am surprised. Noah said he's done a lot in that old house, but the neighbors aren't happy he's living there. They call the cops on him a lot."

That makes me sad.

"Do you think anyone will accept him?"

"Well, you seem to have." Rhianna smirks, lifting her coffee to her lips to try to hide it, but I can see it in her eyes.

"I was just being a decent human," I say defensively.

"He's hot, much hotter than before..." she

says, trailing off.

But I know what she wanted to say... *than before he went to prison.*

"That doesn't mean he's a good person, Rhi. Now, that's enough."

She shrugs but keeps a smirk firmly on her face.

And I wonder, why am I so drawn to August?

CHAPTER 6

A week goes by fast, followed by another. It's lonely. I haven't left the house.

Noah dropped in last week with some essentials, and since then, I haven't left. But I need to because I'm out of food again, and my money stash is becoming smaller with each passing day.

I've never held a real job. Before I went away, I did what was necessary to earn money. It paid, and I never thought beyond that. I probably should have.

There's a small knock on my door, and when I pull it open, I beam. It's the first genuine smile I have had in weeks. Paige is standing on the other side with a bag full of pastries in her hand, and I can smell the delicious treats, which makes my mouth water. All the letters she sent me when I was in prison told me how much she loves to cook, sweets being her favorite. I promised to try them one day in my return letters.

Today must be the day.

"August." She says my name with excitement.

I pull the door open further and she comes inside, her eyes darting around the room before they come back to me. "It's beautiful." She pushes the bag into my hand and goes to the table, running her hand along it. "I made them this morning for you. I hope you like tarts. I've made a few different kinds since I wasn't sure which flavor you liked."

"I do like them. Does your father know you're here?"

She scrunches her nose up and turns her head away, then proceeds to check around the house. I reach for the cell phone Noah gave me, which I haven't used, and send her father a text message letting him know she's here.

"I want you to meet someone..." She pauses. "Beckham. He wants to meet you, too. If you're willing." I can see the hope in her eyes at the mention of his name.

"This your boyfriend?"

"Yes. I love him. He's good to me. Really good." Her smile is so large, her eyes twinkle with the emotion she's feeling.

Who am I to knock that down?

"You're only sixteen, Paige. Don't tie yourself to one person."

"Our mother was sixteen when she had you."

"And look how well that turned out," I say sarcastically.

"I think you turned out great, August." It's the first time someone has said that to me as if I'm not a major disappointment.

I walk over and pat her head before I step into the kitchen and open the bag. The smell hits me straight away, and my mouth starts salivating at the thought of eating the delicious treats right there in front of me. I glance at Paige. "I can have them all?" I ask, hopeful.

Paige giggles. "Of course. I made them for you."

I put one in my mouth and instantly regret not eating enough over the last few days because I know this packet of goodness will be gone before she leaves.

"I can make you more. I bake savory things as well. Beckham prefers them."

"If you cook it, I'll eat it." I wink while stuffing a blueberry tart in my mouth next. She ambles to the living room, which is in front of the open kitchen, and sits, reaching for the remote. She flicks it on and keeps flipping channels.

"Where's your Netflix?" she asks, glancing at me over the back of the couch.

"Don't have it."

Paige gasps then shakes her head. "What do you watch then?"

I shrug. "Nothing."

"You don't watch TV?" she asks, clearly surprised.

"No. I work around the house, then pass out."

Hearing a knock on the front door, I eat the last pastry as I head over to answer it. Glenn stands there, his hands on his trousers which holds his gun, and he's dressed in full uniform.

I had forgotten he's a cop. Well, almost.

Stepping back, I open the door wider. Glenn marches in, offering me a nod before he sees Paige sitting on the couch, still trying to flip through the television channels.

"Paige."

She turns at her father's voice, and her eyes

narrow as she glances at him, then to me. "You told him I was here?" she asks.

"You know you need to ask permission."

Paige stands from the couch, and her hands go up in the air. "He's my brother." Her voice raises as the words leave her mouth. "I should be allowed to see him whenever I want."

I hear Glenn sigh. "Go out front while I speak to August for a moment, please."

She huffs but does as he says, grumbling us as she leaves.

Glenn eyes me up and down. I guess he could be intimidating to some, but I've dealt with a lot scarier people than this man before me. "She's clearly going to keep visiting you."

I nod because we both know it.

He scratches his head then checks outside the door where she's waiting by his cop car.

"Two afternoons a week. If she comes more than that, you have to let me know. Can I trust she will be safe here, August?"

"She'll be safe. You have my word." He turns and calls to Paige, who comes back to the door with a sullen look on her face.

"Two weekdays after school. Don't push your luck," Glenn says to Paige.

She smiles widely and wraps her arms around

her father's waist. "Thank you, Daddy." She beams up at him.

Glenn assesses me while still holding a hand on his daughter. It makes me happy to see she knows what it's like to be loved—something I've never had.

"She is to leave before dinner." I nod at his words.

Glenn leaves, and Paige stays until around six o'clock.

Paige comes over the next day, bringing more food, for which I'm thankful. And that's her limit for that week. But the following week when she comes, she asks me to meet Beckham. She even told me what I should wear. And who the fuck am I to argue with a teenager?

We make our way to the local café where he's meeting us. When we enter, I spot him straight away, only because Paige squeaks next to me as she runs over to him. He hugs her and then pulls her back, offering me his hand as Paige grips herself around him.

"August, I'm Beckham. It's good to meet you." I nod, appreciating how nice his manners are. I, on the other hand, would not have been like him at that age. I slept with them then left them. It was easier.

No attachments.

No problems.

No trouble.

Beckham steps back when I nod, and I see he also brought someone with him. Behind him, sitting at the table is rich girl.

I smirk and pull out the seat opposite her. "Rich girl."

"Prick," she retorts, which only makes my mouth quirk up higher at her sassiness.

"You two know each other?" Paige asks.

"We go way back. But how does your boyfriend know her?"

"That's my brother," Rylee says, clearly confused, and shakes her head.

"You're dating a Harley?" I ask Paige, then look at Beckham. She shrugs. I turn back to Rylee. "How do your parents feel about that? Their son dating a girl who isn't wealthy?"

Rylee simply scoffs before she turns her head away. "How about you guys go and get us some milkshakes while *we* have a chat."

Beckham turns his head to his sister, worry etched on his face, then he spins back to me. I stare him down, waiting for him to speak.

Paige pulls at him, and they stroll away.

"We need to chat?" I ask her, leaning back in my chair.

"Don't be an ass in front of my brother. He's a good kid and loves your sister, asshole."

"Oh, so she does have a backbone. If you do, why does Mommy tell you who you can date?"

Yes, all the town has heard the rumors. The Harley girls are held to high standards, and only one of them has met them until recently. Rhianna is with Noah, and I'm not sure you can do better than him.

Anderson is the scum beneath my feet, and that's where he needs to stay.

"Mommy doesn't tell me who to date, asshole."

"So, you aren't dating Anderson because Mommy wants you to?" My hands sit in front of me. I open them, and her eyes fall down to them before she looks up at me.

"I date Anderson because I want to," she says with venom coating her tone.

"Oh, wow, you chose to date that lowlife. Well, I guess if you chose to, then it's okay, right? You know he cheats on you." She sits back in her chair, and it's as if I slapped her. Hard. She knows, though. We all know. However, why she stays with him? Who knows.

Before she can say another word, her brother pulls out the chair next to her and slides her a shake. Paige does the same, and I smile as I watch Rylee squirm in her seat, and I take great pleasure in doing so.

CHAPTER 7

Rylee

August sits across from me, arrogant and so damn good-looking. I hate that he's so attractive. I loathe it. Because when he speaks to me, butterflies take root in the pit of my stomach, and I can't seem to tame them, even when he's being an ass.

And that's every time I've seen him.

He sits back in his chair, Paige next to him with a wide smile. Beckham glances from Paige to August. I can feel he's intimidated by him. August can be intimidating, but I'm starting to see cracks in his hard exterior. Especially with the way he treats Paige. He respects and loves her. As I do Beckham.

"So, how long you two been dating?" August asks. I sit forward and grin. "Not you, rich girl. We all know that you and that loser have been together way past your expiration date."

Beckham laughs next to me, and I elbow him.

Beckham well and truly agrees with his statement.

"I wasn't going to mention my relationship, but since you seem so interested in it, what else would you like to know?"

"Guys," Paige says, looking between us.

August ignores her and leans forward. I can smell the mint on his breath, and his strong, calloused hands sit between us. Surprisingly, though, his hands are clean.

I have to do my best not to stare at them while imagining those hands roaming every inch of my body.

"Why do you stay? I mean, you do have a mind of your own, and from what I've heard, Anderson isn't all that good in bed." August smirks. He has the audacity to smirk.

I try to contain my expression. But it's hard not to give him my angry face.

"You know how he performs in bed.

Interesting. Never really thought you would care about another man. Unless... you know, prison has changed you..." I say back to him, leaning in as well.

Ha, take that, asshole.

He glances down at my hands, then back up. "Oh, no, not at all. The pleasure of a woman is still what I crave. Would you like to appease me?"

"Guys," Paige says again. "This is awkward as hell. Beckham and I are going to get some ice cream." They stand, and neither of us turns our heads. Both our eyes are pinned on each other.

"No answer, rich girl? Don't want to get your hands dirty by a man who doesn't rely on his mommy and daddy's money?" he teases. He sits back, satisfied with his answer, and crosses his arms over his chest with a gigantic smirk.

"I'm interested... very much so. Why don't you come over here and kiss me?" As soon as the words leave my mouth, I freeze. Because shock then a sly smirk are what creep across August's face. It was simply word vomit, and it came out because I thought he's like Anderson and would just shake his head and laugh at me.

But that was a mistake.

August and Anderson are nothing alike.

Not in the slightest.

August stands, pushes his chair back so hard it tips over, and walks to the seat my brother vacated not too long ago. I watch his strong hands grip the chair and pull it out. Then he sits his ass in it.

Fuck. What have I started?

I can't even run.

Do I even want to, though?

The answer is simple—it's a resounding no.

I would love to know how August kisses. If the rumors about him when we were growing up were true, August was the talk of many women's lips, even mine. And that's just from seeing him from afar.

"Last chance to back out, rich girl." He leans in, vibrant green eyes flick from my lips to my eyes, then back again. I take a deep breath and manage to raise my eyebrows. I can barely hear the people around us as they talk. The noise seems to fade away when I stare at him.

How can I see only him?

When I've been lost in myself for so long?

"Your boyfriend might get jealous," he whispers, all the while leaning closer. I can practically taste him on my lips, that minty smell assaulting my nose. "And I must warn you, I may *not* stop." Again, his eyes pin my lips, and I start to close my eyes as he leans in closer. "I'm a starving man, rich girl, so you better run before I have a taste."

None of his words are registering.

None.

Not one.

I sit waiting, wondering if those lips that are so plump, that tell stories, that call me names, will mark me any second now.

"August."

"Hmm," he replies, clearly not paying any attention to my words now.

I feel the first brush of him, and I'm not fast enough to catch a breath when he touches me.

It was a mistake.

Because when I breathe, I breathe him in, and I think I've become addicted in one single second of him being near me.

Heavenly so.

"Oh my God!" I hear the squeak before his tongue meets mine, and we both pull away at the same time.

"Rylee." I turn to see my brother staring at me. I don't even bother looking at August. I'm stuck on the fact that my lips are pulsing with need for him.

Can you love half-kissing someone?

Because I think I love half-kissing August.

I stand, pushing my chair back.

"I need to go. Do you want a ride?" I ask Beckham.

Beckham turns his attention to Paige, then leans in and kisses her cheek before he nods and steps off. I glance at August, who's watching me with narrowed eyes.

Like he's trying to work me out.

Poison, that's what he is.

My beautiful poison.

And I must stay away.

Men like him aren't right for women like me.

But then again neither is Anderson.

Beckham stays quiet the whole ride home until we pull up to the front of our house. We both sit in silence as we stare at the large, white monstrosity.

"You need to break it off with Anderson," Beckham says. "Not because you kissed another man, but because Anderson has laid his hands on you. And if you don't do something soon, next time he does, I'll come into your room with my bat and beat his fucking head in, and you won't be able to stop me." My mouth hangs open in shock at his words. I watch Beckham as he steps out of the car and hurries to our front door. He's taller than me, the king of his high school, and now almost a man.

When did he grow up?

How did I miss that he isn't my baby brother anymore, but now he's a young man?

I reach for my phone and find Anderson's number. It rings twice before he answers it.

"Babe, what's up?" he says casually.

I grit my teeth as I reply to him, "Let's have dinner tonight. Your favorite restaurant."

"Umm, sure. What's brought this on? You've hardly wanted to see me."

"I'll meet you there," I tell him.

He agrees, then hangs up.

I take a deep breath, knowing that what I am about to do will probably be hard, but I hope that the right setting will ease the conflict.

Hopefully.

\#

I sit at my seat like the perfect possession.

Yes, that's all I am to him.

Nothing more than property he can use and abuse.

My legs are crossed, and my elbows aren't

touching the table as I wait for him to arrive.

He's late. Of course, he is.

I check my phone as the waiter comes back around and offers me a drink.

"Wine, please." He nods and steps off, probably feeling sorry for me.

Ha, don't worry, I feel sorry for me.

No messages and no missed calls. It's going on thirty minutes now, and I'm starving.

Pressing call, Anderson answers, and I can hear the music in the background.

"Where are you?"

"At Larry's, why? What's up, babe?"

"Are you joking?"

This is not going as planned.

I need to end it.

Why is he making this so damn hard?

"We had dinner plans," I huff into the phone.

He goes silent, but the music is pumping in the background.

"Oh, yeah, must have slipped my mind. How about tomorrow night?"

I hang up on him, and the ferocity with which I do it nearly knocks the phone out of my hand. Fuck him!

My phone rings and I answer it without checking. "What?" I bite into the phone.

"Well, fuck! You're mad." I pull the phone away from my ear. It's a number I don't recognize.

"Who is this?"

"August." His voice is husky when he speaks.

"Why are you calling my phone? And how did you get my number?" I ask as my wine arrives. I take the glass and drink it all down in one go. Pity I'm driving, or I would have ordered the whole bottle.

"Paige got it from Beckham. Look... that won't happen again." He makes a guttural sound.

"Okay."

"Okay."

The waiter arrives and asks if I would like to order.

"Where are you?"

"At a restaurant," I tell him, and he goes silent.

"Are you there by yourself?"

"Well, that was *not* the plan."

"So, that's a yes," he answers. "Do they have oysters. Bring me some."

I cough.

"I'm hungry, and I'm sure you are, too. So bring some dinner to my place, rich girl, and I'll keep you company." He hangs up.

My head turns up to the waiter and I order. Then I order for August and ask for it all to be takeout.

What on earth am I doing? Something really fucking stupid, of that I'm sure.

He's standing at the front door naked from the waist up when I arrive. It's dark, but the front porch light is on, and he's hanging some plants from the ceiling. He glances my way, wipes his hands on his jeans that hang dangerously low on his hips, and leans against the side of the house.

He watches me sit in the car, not moving.

I have to talk myself up into actually getting out of the car.

When I check back, he hasn't moved, one hand holding his body up on the wall as the other hangs by his side.

Reaching for our food, I slide out. My heels are sky-high, which makes me as tall as him as I stride toward him. Green eyes stare down at me when I stop at the bottom step. It's a large two-story home, and from what I remember, it didn't look like this. It was run down, and no one had lived in it for years. Now, it's got a fresh coat of paint and could pass for a house in my neighborhood.

"Wow! You have done so much to this old place. I love this."

"Yeah, the wraparound porch is probably my favorite feature of the house. It had a few problems, but nothing a lick of paint and a few nails couldn't fix."

"It's incredible."

"That smells good," August states.

"It does," I reply and shake my head at my words.

August chuckles and reaches for the food, his bare chest coming dangerously close to my arm.

"You smell good, too, rich girl," he whispers near my ear, then turns, taking the food with him as he runs in through the open door. I take a moment, brushing my hand down my soft pink dress, and tread up the stairs following him inside. Shutting the door behind me, my eyes check around. The place is nice. He doesn't have a lot, but it's clean. I can smell the scent of fresh paint everywhere.

"This looks really good," I say, my head turning around in all directions, checking his handiwork.

There's a single three-seater couch that sits in front of the television.

"Nothing compared to what you're used to, I'm sure." I roll my eyes at his comment as I make my way to the kitchen. When I see the pastries, which I know are from Paige, I smile widely.

"She's a good cook, that sister of yours."

August lifts out the steak and gravy, sliding his finger through the gravy and sucking it off his finger. He watches me while he does it.

"I haven't had a steak for years, not one this good anyway."

"I figured you would want more than oysters," I reply as he opens the container filled with oysters.

"Two steaks?" he asks while checking the third container.

I reach for it. "That's mine." I pick it up, which makes him chuckle.

"No salad?" he teases.

"I like steak." Searching around for a knife and fork, I open one drawer and find the utensils. Reaching for two, I give him his while he holds out a plate.

"I like pussy, do you?"

I cough, catching my breath. I take the plate from his hand, and when I look up at him, his eyebrows are raised, and his eyes are dancing with mischief.

"Usually, it's cock that slides into my mouth. Can't say I have had the pleasure of pussy, yet." I slide the juicy steak onto my plate, and when I manage to glance up, I seem to have him frozen in position.

It's as if he's trying to work me out.

"You don't talk to other men this way, do you?"

I wink. "No, my foul mouth only seems to come out just for you."

"I'm sure that's not all that I could make come," he whispers but knows I hear him because he stares at me as he places an oyster into his mouth and sucks it out of the shell, never breaking eye contact.

Glancing away, I take a seat on his couch.

My underwear may be slightly wet.

And my heart is beating erratically.

But it's surprisingly the most comfortable I have been in a long while.

CHAPTER
8

She doesn't seem bothered that my place isn't a palace, which I know is what she's used to. Rylee is used to the finer things in life. I don't think she's ever had to live without them. Her parents are not only some of the wealthiest people in this town, but the country, and she works for them. Rhianna, however, is happy to work at a coffee shop. They are like chalk and cheese.

Rylee works at her father's accounting firm, so I hear, and I also hear she's good.

Stepping over to her, I carry my own food plus

two beers. I place one in front of her, and to my surprise she takes it, pops the top, and puts it to her lips.

"You don't watch much TV?" she asks after taking a sip and setting the bottle down. She cuts into her steak with my blunt-ass knife and puts a piece into her mouth.

"Why do you ask?"

"Because the remote isn't here, unless I'm blind." She checks around before her dark eyes land back on me.

"No, no, I do not. Paige probably takes the thing with her for all I know."

"She would." Rylee giggles and the sound is nice.

"Tell me, rich girl, why are you so dressed up? Were you planning to have dinner by yourself?" I ask, then bite into my steak. It really is a good fucking steak. Best I've ever had.

"I had a date with Anderson."

"Ohhh, Anderson," I say, resisting the urge to call him what he really is.

Fucking scum.

"Yes, but plans changed." She doesn't sound disappointed by that fact.

"Now you have better company," I tell her, reaching for the last bit of her steak and putting it in my mouth.

She opens her pink lips to tell me off, then shakes her head. "Can you put a shirt on?" Her eyes scan my body, and I like it.

"Why?" I ask, swallowing my last bite and placing the plate down next to me.

"Because you have a guest." Her face flushes red.

"And?" I reply, teasing her. "This is my house."

She huffs and stands. Reaching for my plate, she takes them both to the kitchen, her heels clicking on the floor. I hear her cleaning them in the sink, and I'm more than a little surprised she even knows how to do that. Standing, I see her lost in thought, her head down and lips pursed, as she washes circles on the same plate over and over again.

"Why did your plans change with Anderson?" I ask, standing on the other side of the counter. She didn't hear me approach. She's that engrossed in what she's doing.

When she glances up, her eyes, as dark as the night sky, stare at me. A part of me tells me I should look away, that what I see in those dark eyes doesn't pull at every fiber of my being toward her.

But I can't.

I stay, watching her. Waiting for her to answer me.

"He didn't show," she declares with a shrug.

"Told you he was an asshole."

"I already know that," she snaps at me.

"What was dinner for? Special occasion?"

She pulls the plate from the sink into the drainer then places the other in. And when she answers, she doesn't bother to check for my reaction.

"I was trying to call it off, but he won't let me."

Okay, I did *not* expect that.

So I'm glad she can't see the shock on my face.

"You don't love Anderson?"

Now her eyes flash up, a single tear slides down her cheek, but she ignores it and acts like it didn't just fall as she stares at me.

"I thought I did... once." Her voice is filled with such sweet sorrow.

"You're better than him anyway," I tell her. This much I know from one conversation. How he got a girl like Rylee, I'll never know.

I have a feeling she's better than most men around this town.

Even me.

But I'm a selfish man, and even though I should tell her to go, not only because she has a boyfriend, who she clearly wants to leave, but because staring at her is my new favorite thing to do.

The curve of her face is almost heart-like, her lips pink, she tastes like cotton candy, and her eyes, dark as your nightmares.

"You're only saying that because I brought you food." She smirks, the tear falling into the water below as she turns off the running tap.

"Yeah. You can feed me anytime, baby," I say, tapping my stomach. Her eyes fall to it, and her cheeks start to turn pink again.

I like it—a lot.

"How about you show me around. I'm sure you've done more. It's so beautiful." She isn't lying when she says it. She truly thinks my home is beautiful. I don't know how I can tell that, but I just can.

No one has ever said something I've done is beautiful.

Ever.

I run a hand through my hair and smirk. "You want to see the bedroom?" I wait for her to reply.

She puckers her lips and nods her head. "I'd like to see it all. I love older houses. They have so much character." She says it with such enthusiasm.

Rylee wipes her hands on her dress and follows behind me when I turn and head to the stairs. I take the steps slowly, the sound of her heels the only indicator she is behind me as we make our way to the top floor. Opening the bedroom where I sleep, I step to the side so she can enter.

"It smells like you," she says as she steps into my domain. She turns her head back to me over her shoulder and smiles, then spins back. "You seem to like the color brown," she comments, observing my dark stained floors, coupled with a bed I made from scratch last week that is covered with just a plain white sheet. It's the only thing in the room. I haven't had money to waste on bedding, and I don't need much. When I sold my grandmother's bed, I made some money and bought a mattress.

Behind the bed is a wooden feature wall, which I created. She walks over and runs her hand along it.

"I've never seen anything like this before. Even the bed matches." She turns to me. "Did you build all of this?"

"Yes."

"Wow! That's some talent there, Auggie."

I scrunch my nose up at the name she has used.

"My name is August."

"Oh, I know, but I prefer Auggie, it sounds..." she looks up, a mischievous grin playing on her lips, "... cute."

I shake my head. *Cute.* That's not a word to describe me.

We both go quiet as we stare at each other. She runs her hand up her arm, a gesture that she's cold before she speaks again.

"I should get going. I have to work tomorrow."

"You should," I reply. She nods and goes to walk past me, but I don't move. Half of my body blocks the doorway. Rylee sucks in a breath when our bodies touch, and I reach up out of instinct to touch her, the same arm she ran her fingers down earlier, so I do the same.

"I should..." She doesn't finish her sentence as I move my fingers back up her arm and the crease of her elbow. Goosebumps prickle on her skin as my fingers ever so slightly touch her stomach.

"You should," I say back to her.

She leans into me slightly, and I open my mouth as she does. I know what she wants. "I'll be seeing you, rich girl," I say, dropping my hand away from her and stepping back so she can leave. It takes her only a moment to realize what was about to happen before she treads down my stairs, and I hear the front door shut, followed by the start of her car.

"That was weird," Paige says as she steps into my house the next day after school. She throws her bag on the floor, walks into the kitchen, and automatically starts baking. I bought her some essentials that she asked for, and the rest she brought over a few weeks ago.

"What?" I say as I'm washing my hands. She makes me help, but just with the small things.

"Don't play dumb." She gives me her teenager eye roll. I laugh and shake my head, passing her the mixer. A knock is heard on the front door and Paige is first to bounce off to open it. I grab the cupcake tray and place it on the counter for her.

She's quiet. I can't hear any voices.

The hairs on the back of my neck raise when I make my way to the front door.

Paige is standing there smiling at Josh.

Josh, the scum of the fucking earth.

"Paige, get back to cooking." She turns back to me, her smile fading, but she does as I say. When she's gone, I stalk over to him and step outside, shutting the door behind me.

"What the fuck are you doing here?" I ask. He opens his mouth then his lips turn up.

It's fake, just like him. His silver grills sit on his bottom teeth, and he licks them.

"Is that any way to greet an old friend?" the bastard has the audacity to ask.

"Fuck off," I seethe, leaning in. "And if you ever come back, I will fucking kill you."

"Now, now, now, August boy." He's always called me that. He's only ten years older than me, but he acts like I'm some stupid fucking teenager.

Wrong.

I worked for Josh on the streets, selling, breaking into places for him. He paid me well, until the last job that sent me away for good.

It was a job that was meant to be easy.

But when I turned up and saw two of his other men there, I got cold feet. They called me a pussy and put a gun to my head, telling me I had no damn choice.

Robbery.

In the end, it was a set-up.

They broke into the store, marched me to the cold room, and locked me in there, destroying the place and taking everything they could.

I was found in the cold room with a gun on the floor next to me.

The bastards had called the cops on me.

Those bastards set me up.

Josh denies it all to this day.

In court, they told the judge that it was me

who had a gun to their head and made them do it.

They got parole.

I got prison.

Turns out, they stole a lot of money, and the shop was owned by a government official.

Just my fucking luck.

"I'm not your boy, Josh," I spit back at him. "Now *fucking* leave."

"That your little sis in there?" He nods. "She's a cute little thing," he says with that evil fucking smirk of his.

"I am not kidding, Josh." I step up closer. "Don't come around here again or anywhere near her."

"Your mom asked me to come around," he says, that awful smirk never leaving his damn fuck ugly face. "Told me to tell you she wants you to come visit."

Drugs and alcohol fucked her up early on when I was a kid. It's how I met Josh to begin with. I worked for him to pay back her debt, then he offered me more money than I could refuse. It's hard when you're a teenager and have nothing and someone offers you something for jobs you know are wrong but you need food.

And I needed food.

I turn and reach inside, grabbing the bat I keep by the door. I swing back around to see he is no longer on the porch. Now he's standing near his car, his hand up in the air.

"I'll be seeing you, August boy."

CHAPTER
9

Rylee

Anderson ignores me all week. Oh, he calls and texts, but not once does he make an effort to come and see me. So when Friday comes around, I know I have to go see him because clearly, he isn't coming to me.

Pulling up to where I know he is—at a party, as usual—I walk in with people staring at me. I'm dressed in my work clothes because I couldn't be bothered to stop at home to change. I need to do this now, or I'm afraid it'll never happen.

One of Anderson's friends spots me first. His eyes go wide with the realization that I'm here because I never come to these things. Getting drunk every weekend does not interest me. Sometimes you have to grow up, and clearly, Anderson doesn't know how to.

"Hi, Blade," I say to him while checking around for Anderson. Then I spot the fucker walking out with a girl by his side. His eyes flick to me, then flare, before he strides my way. His hand goes to my waist, and he pulls me out the front door and away from everyone.

I go because I need to speak to him.

His hand is tight on my arm, and I shake it off once we get outside.

I look up, then take a step back.

"You have a little something right there." I tap the side of my mouth. "Lipstick." I smirk. "Thank you so very much for making this easier. Don't contact me anymore. I'm telling my parents I have called it off. This..." I wave between us, "... is off." I watch as he takes my words in. His face changes from confused to shocked, and finally to anger. His eyebrows are pinched, and his lips pursed as he stares at me with furious eyes.

"You don't get to call that."

"I do." I step back again.

The front door opens and a girl steps out. Her

hand goes to her belly. She's the same girl who was standing next to him when I arrived. "Your new flavor of the month is searching for you," I say, glaring at him.

He steps forward, grabs hold of my arm again, and holds it tight. "Rylee, you don't get to choose. Haven't you figured that out since I first cheated on you? It's a weekly event. Don't act like it's affecting you now," he snarls while his fingers dig deeper into my arm. I know it's going to bruise, and I'll have to hide them too.

"Get..." I say silently, "your hands *off of me.*" I raise my voice for that last part. "Before I scream," I say when he doesn't drop them.

Finally, he does, and I step farther back.

"Rylee, you can't escape me. We are destined."

"Bullshit! Now lose my number," I say as I rush away and get into my car, only checking back once to see if he's following me. Thankfully, the other girl is keeping him occupied.

Driving away, my hands shake on the steering wheel. As soon as I see a park, I pull over to give my shaking hands and beating heart a chance to rest.

My phone starts ringing, but I ignore it. Clenching my hands, I try to stop the shaking that is taking over my entire body from what I just did.

I just ended something that has been a part of my life since high school.

It was well overdue, but that doesn't make doing it any easier.

It's hard.

But necessary.

Anderson, despite being the cheating prick he is, and the abusive asshole he's become, was there for me for many years. Yes, he may have shown sympathy in times of need for his own agenda, but he was there for me.

A part of me loved him. It's why I stayed so long when I really should have walked away years ago.

My phone blares again, and when I pick it up to check, I see it's my sister.

"Ry, gosh, where are you?"

"Driving."

"Okay, well, drive your ass here, would ya?"

It's where I was going anyway since home is not an option right now. And Anderson wouldn't dare come near me around Rhianna. He knows she will *not* take his shit.

Managing to catch my breath and stop my shaking hands, I drive to Rhianna's to see her already at the front door. Her hands are crossed, and she is in her pajamas as she stands there waiting for me.

Closing the car door, I make my way to her.

"Anderson tried calling me. And we all know the only reason that would be is because you finally broke it off with him," she says with a gigantic smirk. "I'm glad. Really happy for you, Ry."

I rub my hand up my arm where he grabbed hold. It's hurting badly. "It was long overdue."

"Yes, very much so. Now come… let's go and kick Noah out of my bed, and you can tell me how your week has been." She hooks her arm through mine as we step inside.

"I can't kick your boyfriend out of your bed. I'll sleep on the couch," I say quietly, so we don't wake Noah.

"Nah, he won't care. And he knows you're always first, Ry, no matter what. Do you get that?"

Her bedroom door opens, and Noah rushes out dressed in only boxers, rubbing his eyes when he sees us.

After looking straight at Rhianna, he says, "I'll take the couch." We watch as he goes back in, grabs a pillow, then lies down on the couch with no hesitation.

"Told you," she says as she pulls me to her

bedroom. It's where I sleep when I stay. We shared a bed through most of our childhood. Even though we had our own, one way or another, we would always end up in bed together. It wasn't until I started seeing Anderson that it changed, and Rhianna moved out. Then I started to come to her house when everything was too much.

I pull my cardigan off my body and kick my shoes away before I climb into bed with her.

"You're bruising," Rhianna says, gently touching my arm. When I check, it's red, and a light purple is starting to come through. "So, it didn't go well?"

"Better than I thought."

If I'm honest with myself, I expected to walk out with worse than a sore, bruised arm. But she doesn't need to know that.

"I hate him," she says and rolls onto her back and stares at the ceiling. "If I could get away with it, I would put rat poison in that bastard's coffee and kill him." She works at a coffee shop and dreams about all the ways to kill Anderson, and she's come up with some doozies over the years.

I laugh at her.

"I'll pretend I didn't hear that," Noah calls from the living room.

We both crack up laughing, knowing full well

he's a lawyer, and if she was put on trial for murder, he would get her off. He's simply that good.

"You hush, or I'll put it in *your* morning coffee," she says back to Noah, making him groan. He knows she would never do that. I have never seen my sister so smitten in my life.

And she picked a great one to be smitten with, that's for sure.

"I heard something…" Rhi says, turning so we are both lying on our sides facing each other. "Well, Vicki did." Vicki is Rhianna's roommate and best friend.

"Yeah?"

"That Anderson knocked up a girl," she whispers.

My mouth opens, and my eyebrows rise at her words.

"He'll do anything to get rid of it," I say. "His family believes marriage before kids, and he does whatever they say like a good little boy."

"Yeah, supposedly she went to his parents first, and she's past her first trimester."

I go to speak, but words fail me.

Why would he not have told me?

How come no one told me?

"I don't understand." A tear slips down my

cheek.

She wipes it away fast as if it wasn't even there.

"Did he expect to keep me as well as her?" I ask, confused.

"I would make a solid bet on that. Absolutely he would think that way."

"He was with a girl tonight, actually..." I try to remember her appearance. "She had her hand on her belly when she came outside. I just assumed she was cold."

"Yeah, well, his mommy and daddy are not happy, so we hear."

"When did you find out?"

"Tonight. Vicky told me, and when I managed to wrap my head around it, I figured you would be asleep, but then he called. I didn't answer."

"How long has he known?"

"For a few weeks," she says.

That would explain why he's eased off on the pressure of a ring after that night he came to my room.

How dumb can I be?

Really.

"I need to move."

"Yeah, you kind of do," she says, sliding her hand into mine next to me. "Vicki might be moving in with her boyfriend, so you want to live with me?"

My first thought is to say no, but then…

"Yes. Yes, I do."

"Good. It's a done deal. I'll tell her tomorrow."

I lay my head on her shoulder, and she runs her fingers through my hair as I fall asleep.

I wake to Rhianna curled on her side, still asleep. I manage to get out of the bed without waking her and quietly make my way out of the room. When I get to the kitchen, Noah is at the counter, a coffee in his hand as he reads something on his phone. When he turns, he smiles. "Coffee?" he asks.

"I'll get it." He nods and checks his phone again. I fix a cup and give him a sideways glance. "You love her, right?" I know it's a silly question, but I need to hear it.

He places his phone down and gives me his full attention. "With every breath I take. She's it. The crazy and all."

"She's pretty special."

"And so are you. You both are extraordinary…" He pauses as I pour my milk. "I can file restraining orders if need be. Just let me know." He nods to my arm.

I flinch when I see the black and purple ringing my forearm. Guess I'll be wearing cardigans until the bruising is gone.

"August mentioned you helped him," he says when I bring my drink to my lips. "Thanks for that. He wouldn't have liked it, but I'm sure he's appreciative."

"He wasn't," I reply, remembering how mad it made him that I bought his groceries.

Noah chuckles. "Give him time. He isn't the monster people paint him to be."

Rhianna comes out of the bedroom, then steps up behind Noah and wraps her arms around his neck.

"No rat poison in that coffee now, is there?" she says with a wink at me.

I can't help the laughter that leaves my mouth, and it's genuine. More so than I have felt for a long time. My happiness has been something no one cared about, even me.

"Woman, you aren't making my coffee anymore," he says, pulling her around so she is practically in his lap.

"Oh, hush, you. I don't want you dead... yet. I need you for the orgasms."

"Priorities." He chuckles at her words. I look away because, no matter how much I love them, I'm also jealous of what they have.

CHAPTER 10

August

I never really had any true friends before I was locked away. People only hung around me for popularity or drugs. I had both, and they all wanted it. So it was no surprise when I got locked up that I never heard from any of them. But as I stand in front of Sully with my hands full of food, I can't help when my face turns into a scowl.

He was the only one I assumed would be there, who would at least write. I had known him the longest. We'd been friends all through school.

"August," he says and gives me a once-over with his eyes. I'm dirty from finishing up the backyard this week. I had to fucking do something after rich girl left because no matter how many times I stroked my fucking cock, it didn't do me any good.

Her pink lips wrapped around it is what it wanted.

"Sully." I nod and step around him to begin my walk home, not giving him the time he clearly didn't want to give me. I hear his footsteps and then see him next to me. He hasn't changed much since I last saw him, still tanned with blond hair. I had originally put him in that pretty-boy category, but he fell out of it when I realized I liked who he was as a person.

"I didn't know you were out."

Not stopping my pace, I squint my eyes and face forward.

We've stepped out of the shopping area. I might add it was a lot easier to make my purchases this time than last time because asshole rent-a-cop must have had a day off.

"You live locally?"

He doesn't ask if I am back with my druggy mother, even though I know that's what he wants to know.

Again, I don't answer him.

"August, can you stop, so I can talk to you?"

I huff. Stop. Then turn to face him. Not speaking.

Sully scratches his head and gives me a sort of smile. "Thanks, man. I've been trying to see you." It's a lie, but I don't want to argue about a moot point, so I turn around and keep walking. "Fuck, man, I have."

"You don't owe me anything, Sully. Now, fuck off." I hear his footsteps stop, but I don't slow down. As I walk down my street, I see a very attractive woman sitting on my bottom step. When she notices I am there, I swear I see a glitter in those dark eyes.

"Rich girl." I smile because I simply can't help myself. She is perfect. And a very nice sight after Sully.

"Hey, hope you don't mind I popped around. I left my jacket here."

"Come in," I tell her, opening the door and stepping inside. I nod to where her jacket is on the back of the couch, and she reaches for it, then turns back to face me.

"You went shopping?" she asks, surprised.

"Yep, a man's got to eat."

She nods.

"You want to stay for dinner, rich girl?" Her dark eyes fall back to me, and I smirk at her.

"I mean... you do owe me." She places her jacket down again and heads over to the counter. I open the fridge and hand her a beer. She takes the bottle from my outstretched hand, opens it, and places it to her mouth.

Damn, the things I could do with that mouth...

"You sure Anderson won't get upset you're here?"

"No. There's no more Anderson."

Well, fuck, her words surprise me. I raise an eyebrow, and she simply shakes her head.

"So now you can spend your time with the less fortunate," I say, playing with her. She opens her mouth to defend herself against my words but shuts it and takes another drink instead.

"I want you to kiss me," she blurts out.

"I don't kiss girls like you."

"You have," she says defensively, holding her head high, the beer clutched firmly in her hand.

I smirk and shake my head as I get the pasta out and put some water on to boil.

"No, I did it to amuse myself. That wasn't a real kiss. That was nothing more than a child's kiss," I answer. When I turn back, she is assessing me with her brows scrunched together, her eyes stuck on me but not really seeing me.

"You don't want to kiss me?"

I drop the pasta in boiling water and move around the counter until I'm standing next to her. She turns ever so slightly and tilts her chin up.

"It's not those lips I would kiss." Her face turns bright red, and she quickly turns her head away, bringing her drink to her lips. I lean in, so I'm close to her ear. "And we both know you don't want me to do that. Not a dirty man like me," I say to her with a bite of venom in my voice. I watch her shudder before I resume cooking.

"Paige been around this week?" she asks, changing the subject.

"What are you doing here, rich girl. You got no friends?" My voice is harsh, and I don't check for her reaction. "Am I the only one who puts up with you?"

"You offered to feed me, August," she bites back.

"Okay, yeah, you're right." I focus back on cooking. I hear her finishing off her beer and she grabs another one.

"Who taught you to cook?"

"The internet," I tell her truthfully. The

things my mother taught me to cook are not what a child should be anywhere near.

"You aren't close to your mother?"

I dish up our food, after adding bacon and garlic to the pasta, then slide hers over to her.

"Why are you asking so many questions?" I bite back as she puts her fork in the pasta and twirls it around.

"How come you don't like sharing?"

"Eat your food and leave, rich girl. I'm sure you have places to be rather than here, annoying me." I glance up to see her pushing her plate away. She's finished half of it.

"I do, actually. I need to move. You free tomorrow?"

"Are you requesting my services or telling me to make myself available?" My head drops to the side. "Because you're shit at asking."

She shakes her head with her eyes slightly closed before she stands and walks around to my side of the counter. She steps to me, only leaving a foot of space between us as she smirks. "August, I would love your manly help tomorrow to move all my *big* items." She flutters her eyelashes at me.

I know she's doing it as a joke, but my cock appreciates all that effort.

"Sure."

She claps her hands together, kisses my cheek, and quickly turns around. Grabbing her things, she throws her bag over her shoulder as she heads for the door. "I'll pick you up."

CHAPTER 11

Rylee

August lifts my mattress, and I can't help but stare at his bulging muscles. I really should be doing something else besides watching him carry all my things inside.

I really should.

But it's so hard to look away.

So I don't.

Anderson never had a body like this. Sure, he was fit, but not to the point you could see the veins in his hands whenever he moved them.

I like veins in men's hands now.

I like a lot of new things.

August being the main thing.

Like the side stink-eye he gives me every time he catches me watching him. He never speaks of it, just continues on with whatever he's doing.

August said a quick, gruff hello, and that's all I have gotten out of him all day since I picked him up. He's dressed in dark blue jeans with a light blue shirt that continually rides up, giving me an eyeful of his toned stomach, every time he picks up something new.

I have carried all my small things up already, and now it's just the bigger items that need placement around the place. I offered help, but he turned me down.

So I lean against the back of my borrowed truck and simply watch him.

"You really should remove your shirt. It's only getting in the way," I tell him, bringing the straw of my drink to my lips and taking a sip before I let anything else slip out.

August's hands go to his shirt, and in a quick movement, he has it off and over his head, then he throws it at my face. I giggle as I pull it away and see him already going on to the next thing.

"Oh, I didn't know we signed up for a strip show. Noah, you should do that, too." I turn to see Noah shaking his head at my sister as he walks by helping August.

August speaks to him, not in any manner he speaks to me, and I watch, fascinated.

"Ummm, what's going on?" Rhianna asks, and I turn to see her staring at me.

"What?"

Her eyes fall to where the boys just disappeared then back to me. "You're staring awfully hard at the man in blue."

I blush and shake my head at her words.

"I asked him to help. He's helping."

"Anderson hasn't been around?"

"Nope."

"Good. You don't need that. But we both know who he is..." She pauses. "Just be careful. Because if he sees you with him..." she nods when August walks out, "... I'm not sure I'd like the outcome."

I'm not sure I would either. It's not that we think August couldn't take on Anderson. No, we know that for sure he would have no problem. But Anderson has connections that could throw August straight back where he doesn't want to be. Prison. And I would hate to think I had anything to do with that.

"Don't stop being 'friends' with him. Noah said it's good for him to get out."

"Noah his daddy now?" I joke with her.

"No, but I have a feeling he is his only friend." She nudges me. "Apart from you now, of course."

"You two seem to be working hard," Noah says, lifting his shirt and wiping his face.

The truck is now empty, and my lips turn up as August walks over to us.

"I'm treating for dinner, as a thank you," I tell him, then look at my sister and Noah for confirmation.

"We can't. Noah has a business thing tonight, and I'm going to keep him company. But you two should go."

When I glance at August, he's not even paying attention to me. He's closing up the truck and doing his very best to ignore me. Turning back to my sister, I smile before Noah wraps his arms around her and they head inside the apartment.

"Dinner?" I ask as August closes the door, and his green eyes find mine.

"I need to change."

"You can take my car and come back when you're ready." I throw my keys to him. August catches them and glances down at them as if they are on fire before he looks back at me.

"You trust me with your car?" I can't help but notice the surprise in his intonation.

"Should I not?"

"I could steal it, sell it off for parts."

"Okay, umm… you're really not selling yourself here." I laugh.

"Why do you trust me with your car?" he asks, pushing me a little harder.

"It's just a car."

He shakes his head, steps toward me, and tries to hand the keys back but I don't take them. "I can find my own way home."

"No, take the car, August. And come back for dinner. I'll even order in if you want."

"You want me to stay for dinner?"

"Yes. Now go, because you really do stink." I push him away from me. I know he has his license, Noah told me, so I know he can drive, but the way he inspects the keys, you would think he's won the Willy Wonka Golden Ticket.

"I've never willingly taken a car like this for a drive unless it was stolen," he says, smirking. "Should I drive it like it's stolen, too?" he asks when he opens the door.

"You're making me rethink this."

He laughs, gets in, and starts the ignition. The window comes down, and he looks good in it.

"I'll treat her real fiiine." He winks before he pulls out.

Why, oh why, did those words hit something deep inside me?

He's on time. I like that about him. He steps inside and past me, handing me the keys on the way. He smells fresh, and his hair is still wet.

While he was gone, I managed to tidy up some things and get them in order. I didn't have to do much, just some bedding, which I bought brand-new, plus a dresser. All my other stuff I brought in the back of my car, and my sister and Noah helped bring the rest in their car as well. But I couldn't carry it all by myself, and I could've paid for a mover, but being around August does something to me.

I like him.

A lot.

"Your parents own this place?" he asks, coming to sit at the table as I order food from my laptop.

"Indian?" I ask, to which he nods. "Yes. Rhianna wanted to move out. She and my mother clash a lot, so this was a happy medium," I say, closing the laptop. "Thank you for your help today."

"I'll think of a way you can pay me back."

"Well, you think on that and let me know." I wink, standing and walking to the fridge. I pull out a bottle of wine I bought earlier, and grab two glasses, bringing it all back to the table. "You drink wine?"

"Do you intend to get me drunk, rich girl?" he asks as his arms come up on the table, crossing over one another. My eyes naturally go to his muscled hands and cross my legs.

"That wasn't my intention, but now that you mention it, getting you drunk could be fun."

"You really don't know what you're doing, do you? I'm not someone you want to be with. Is it amusing to you?" he asks. "To want me? And don't even deny it, I see the way you stare at me." I try to keep my cheeks from going pink, but there's no way that's going to happen.

"Why aren't you someone I might want?" I manage to ask back.

"Because girls like you go for guys like Noah, not men like me." His eyes lock on mine. "I'm bad for you. I would taint you, and you would enjoy it to the point where you keep coming back for more because you couldn't stop when we both know you should."

"You think a lot of yourself there, Auggie." I smirk widely, and he scrunches up his face at the nickname.

"I know, I've seen it. Usually, it ends badly, and it's not the little rich girl who gets hurt in the situation. It's the poor guy who warned her." He sits back, his hands disappearing under the table.

I hang on to his words and pour us each a glass of wine, sliding his over to him. I lift mine and drink, staring at him over the rim of the glass through my eyelashes. He doesn't reach for his but watches me instead.

Placing the glass down, I tap the rim of it. "I'm

more than some little rich girl. I've worked for everything I have. I paid for that car. I'll be paying to live here. Yes, my family has money, and yes, I have benefited from that. But that does *not* mean I am any less or better than you."

"What do you want from me, rich girl?" he asks. "Honestly. What do you want? You keep coming around, and you keep calling. What do you want?"

I pour myself another glass of wine and gulp it down, then look him straight in the eye. "I want *you.*"

His fingers tap on the table, then he stands. At first, I think he's about to head straight out the door, but he comes to stand directly in front of me instead. He reaches down and moves the glass out of the way and puts his finger under my chin, tilting my head up to him.

"You just want to fuck. You don't want me."

"Why don't you fuck me then?" I breathlessly whisper.

He smirks, and my heartbeat picks up.

"Just fucking?"

"Just fucking," I repeat his words.

He leans down to kiss me, his lips brushing mine ever so slightly. I sit up straighter so I can taste him. But he doesn't let me. Only the softest of touches is all he's permitting.

I want him.

I need him.

My heart beats fast, my legs quiver with need, and my hands want to pull him by his hair so he has no choice but to kiss me thoroughly.

Kiss me, goddamn you.

"Rich girl," he says, his lips still brushing mine.

"Hmmm…" is all I manage.

"Goodnight," he says, then pulls away.

I'm too shocked to stop him, to tell him to come back.

Does he not want me? Because I know I want him.

I run out the door just in time to see him running down the street.

"Asshole," I yell.

I hear his chuckle as he sprints away.

"Fuck," I whisper.

The man keeps turning me down, and I keep coming back like some sort of addicted drug addict.

What is it about August that grips me so?

Because I sure as shit know it's not his damn personality. Asshole, tease that he is.

Stripping, I climb into the shower and try to rid myself of his lips.

It's useless.

He's all I dream about when I finally fall into a fitful sleep.

CHAPTER 12

August

"August."

I turn at the sound of my name and see my mother standing on the other side of the street. Seeing her was bound to happen, eventually. But I didn't expect it to be tonight. I guess that's what I get for choosing to walk home instead of fucking Rylee every which way to Sunday.

The old bitch crosses the street, and I can tell straight away she's drunk. Her feet are unstable, and her eyes are glassy. Alcohol is her chosen poison, but that's not to say she doesn't love to dabble in everything there is that she can afford. It's one of the reasons I started working for Josh all those years ago, to keep her in alcohol and drug money.

"August, baby, oh God… look at you." She reaches out to touch my face, but I step back so she can't touch me. "August, what's wrong? Haven't you missed me?"

No, not in the fucking slightest.

I don't answer her. Instead, I turn and continue my path home.

"I heard you got mother's house. You should sell it. We could use that money." Hence the reason my grandmother never left it to her. "August, don't you ignore me, son."

When I don't answer her again, she says, "Oh, come on, August, why are you being so rude to your mother?" I turn to see Josh leaning on his car, right next to my mother. Of course, they're together.

A car pulls in front of me. It's Rylee. She glances at me, then to my mother, who's staring at her car. "Get in." I do because the alternative is not what I want. "You know her?" she asks as she pulls away.

Josh watches us go with a smirk on his face.

"No."

"Okay," she says. "Look, I'm sorry for… before." She doesn't go into any more detail. I can see she's showered, and she smells like strawberries.

Now I'm craving strawberries.

"What? For asking me to fuck you?"

She gasps at my bluntness, and her hands squeeze the steering wheel tightly. She's dressed in what appears to be a long shirt. I can't help but check out her legs.

"Why did you come?"

"I realized you didn't have a ride. It was rude of me to let you leave, considering you don't live around the corner."

We sit in silence as I stare out the window.

"That was my mother," I tell her as we arrive at my house.

"You aren't close?"

"No. She's an alcoholic and a druggie. So no, I stay away from her. Far away."

Rylee comes to a stop, and I get out of her car. Closing the door, I walk around to hers and open it. "Come in."

"I don't have shoes on. I ran to the car from the shower." She touches her wet hair, and I realize she didn't even dry it. The back of her shirt is soaked.

"Get out of the car, rich girl," I command.

She turns the car off and steps one foot out, followed by the other. I bend and put my arms under her knees, then pick her up so she doesn't have to walk barefoot to the front door. She squeals when I do it but places her arms around my neck as I carry her bridal-style to the front of the house.

"Do you know why you're coming in?" I ask, glancing down at her. I like the feel of her in my arms, so much so that I don't want to put her down when we get to the door. But of course, I do.

"I have no idea with you anymore," she replies truthfully.

As soon as the front door is unlocked, I reach for her face, sliding my hands on either side of it and touching my lips to hers. She opens with need the minute my tongue demands attention, and I shift backward, lifting her so her feet wrap around my waist. I feel her ass underneath her shirt and squeeze it as I kick the door shut.

She moans into my mouth but refuses to break contact.

Jesus, can she kiss.

Why did I wait so long?

Because I knew I would become addicted.

Is one taste ever enough?

I'm obsessed with the girl whose eyes are as black as the night sky and a voice that entrances me.

Her hands grip the back of my neck hard, her nails digging into my skin, but I don't stop her.

She's the first woman I've been with for a long time. So rushing it is not something I want to do. And I had made my mind up it wouldn't be with her.

I place Rylee on my couch. She lets go of my neck, unhooks her legs from my waist, and pulls her T-shirt dress over her head. She's wearing no bra and only a pair of black lace panties.

Her lips are pink with need, and she bites her bottom one as she stares at me. I reach for my shirt, pulling it over my head, and kick off my shoes.

"Only sex."

She doesn't answer.

"Rich girl, tell me you heard me." My hands pause on my belt buckle.

She sits up, her tits are bigger than I thought they were, and I want to fuck them, along with every other part of her body.

She reaches for my jeans and pulls my cock out, her soft hands choking it ever so perfectly before she leans forward and places her tongue on the tip. She circles and then in one swift movement, like she was made for me, she takes me fully into her mouth, her hand at the bottom pumping while her other fondles my balls.

Reaching for her hair, I grip tight, not directing because she clearly doesn't need that but to hold the fuck on for dear life.

It doesn't take long for me to explode, and I'm glad it was in her mouth for my first time, rather than her pussy.

Because that pussy, well that, I plan to fuck all fucking night.

She wipes her mouth and pulls back. Her smirk is well and truly in place as she stands in front of me, my jeans now kicked off somewhere in between everything that's happening.

"I heard you," she states. "But you may become addicted." She winks and pulls me down so I am sitting on the couch.

My hands touch her back and slide up. *Fuck, her skin is like silk.* Wrapping my hands around her as she comes to sit on me, my cock instantly hardens as I feel her wet heat. I kiss her neck, and she drops her head back and starts sliding over me. My cock is not in her pussy, but I'm very much enjoying the feeling of her slick warmth rubbing along my shaft.

She lifts her hands and runs her fingers through her hair as I lean forward and kiss my way to her tits. And just as I thought, they taste so fucking sweet.

I like that she thinks she has control, and I'm allowing her to think that because I don't know her well enough to know her limits. So I let her glide herself against me until she stops. When I move my mouth away from her tits, I slip my hand down between us, positioning my cock for her to slide on.

She licks her lips, then she slowly drops down, taking it at her own pace, her pussy clenching around my cock.

I'm amazed I don't come again. Instead, I lean forward and grip her to me tight, and stand with her, while she wraps her arms around me, then walk her to the counter. Pulling her hands free, I lay her down so her bare back is on the countertop and skim my hand up between her breasts to her neck and give it a slight squeeze to keep her in place.

"Do you want me to fuck you, rich girl?" I lean forward, pinning her in place, and bite her nipple.

"Yes," she moans.

"Tell me, rich girl. Tell me you want me to fuck you." It takes everything in me not to slam into her right now. Not to fuck her until we are both sore and unable to move.

I started having sex at fifteen with a girl who most would consider was from the wrong side of town. She was older and knew so much more than me. Then, when I was sixteen, I moved on to a different type. Older women. I liked to fuck older women. They knew what they wanted and didn't ask for anything more.

It was easy.

So easy.

Rich girl is not going to be easy.

No, when I glance down into those devil-worshipping eyes, I know she'll be anything but easy.

"Fuck me, August."

I smirk at her words.

No Auggie this time.

So, I do as she says. I hold her in place and fuck her cunt until she's screaming with everything she has.

And then I keep going because I fucking can.

CHAPTER 13

I had read somewhere that a man falls in love faster than a woman. A man can fall in love at first sight, whereas a woman can take up to three months, sometimes longer. And that a man is more inclined to wait for the woman to mutter those *three little words* first.

I don't know how true that is, but with August, I know he could never love me. He looks at me as if I'm the devil.

But I'm also okay with that.

I accept it because I like him.

He picks me up like a rag doll as I lie helplessly on the kitchen counter. He left me lying there and grabbed a bottle of water, drinking it down, then grabbed another before throwing me over his shoulder.

My legs are sore. And between my legs, there is a dull ache. But the bounce in his step makes me believe he's neither. He walks with me hanging over him up the stairs to his room, kicks the door open, deposits me on the bed, then hands me the bottle of water. I take it, drinking while he watches me.

"So, your mother is a sore spot, then?"

He shakes his head but doesn't answer, then heads into the closet, grabbing a fresh pair of underwear.

"Do you want a pair?" he asks, completely ignoring my initial question.

I sit up on my elbows and let my eyes soak him in. His body is defined in every possible way. He has that V cut, which connects to his perfectly shaped penis, which I might add is the perfect size, soft and hard. And, he made me come from his cock alone. Anderson had never been able to do that. Ever. So I assumed it was a myth. How wrong was I?

"Do you want to shower before I fuck you again?" he asks since I've ignored his previous question because my eyes are too lost glancing over his body. I manage to lift my eyes to his chest, which I've seen before, but the sight of it still makes me want to get off the bed and run my hands down the taut bumps and grooves, leaving fingernail impressions as I go.

"What about in the shower?" I ask, sitting up. "I've never had sex in the shower."

"How is that possible?"

I shrug, not wanting to get into it that Anderson only liked to fuck me doggy style.

"Shower it is then." He steps out and I follow. I ogle his naked ass until he reaches the bathroom and runs the shower. He places two towels down and steps in, holding the shower curtain open for me. It's an old shower over a bath. I step in as he moves under the stream and lets the water run down his body. The droplets of water run over the muscles and then continue down his body, and for some reason, it makes me parched. It's as if I'm in the Sahara Desert, and the only water available is on him.

Fuck, my arousal level has skyrocketed just from staring at him.

Again, how can that be possible?

Stepping up to him, my hands play on his firm stomach, not reaching his cock this time but watching as it hardens at my touch.

He makes me feel powerful, wanted,

desired. His body wants me, even if his mind isn't sure it does.

"What kind of women were you with before me?" I ask, tracing the lines on his stomach, fascinated with his V.

His hands drop to his sides, letting me touch him however I want.

"Not ones like you," he answers coldly.

His hand reaches up and wraps around my neck, and I turn around. He pushes forward while my ass presses back into him.

"Turn back around. I like to watch your soulless eyes when I fuck you." I do as he says and press my front into him. He grips me by the neck again with one hand and puts the other under one leg, hiking it up and bringing me forward so our bodies are entirely touching. "You *will* look at me as I make you come. No closing your eyes."

I nod as he bends his knees ever so slightly and slides straight into me. As he enters me I gasp but keep my eyes open, like he requested. I reach up and wrap my arms around his neck as he lifts me fully, so now we're fucking standing up.

My back hits the cold wall, and he lets go of my ass as I grip onto him for dear life with my legs and glide up and down. His hands are now sliding into my own hands, entwining our fingers before he pulls them up the wall so I'm being held up by them. I don't let go of my grip around his waist with my legs and, somehow, I keep on managing to move. I can feel the orgasm building, wanting to claim me as much as I want it to.

"Open those eyes," he whispers, then bites my neck.

I do, and when I glance at him with hooded eyes, his green ones don't leave mine. He wants to see it all, watch me as I start to come undone. And I don't feel the need to look away, to feel embarrassed or ashamed. No, this feels amazing. It's as if I am all that he wants right now.

"That's it," he says, leaning in and giving me an open-mouthed kiss as I come. I kiss him back, and he lets go of my hands and grips my ass to keep me from falling while he keeps fucking me.

I like being fucked by August Trouble.

Very much so.

He left me to shower alone, and when I step out, I find my clothes sitting on the sink. I get dressed quickly and head downstairs to find him making himself a sandwich in the kitchen.

"You want one?"

"No, I should be going..."

"Bye."

One word.

That's all he says.

One single word.

Then he turns his bare back to me. There's a towel wrapped around his waist, hiding that gorgeous ass from me, but I can see the outline.

I make my way to the door but stop before I open it. When I peek back over my shoulder, he's watching me.

"Don't make it out to be more than what it was, rich girl. It was just sex."

"It was," I lie.

He smirks as if he knows I'm lying. Grabbing my keys from my handbag, I pull it over my shoulder and turn to leave. The whole drive home, my mind replays every single scene, as if it's a movie playing rent-free in my head.

Was that a stupid thing to do? I mean, technically, it's only been a few weeks since I split from Anderson, even though I'd been trying to get rid of him for a lot longer. I was with Anderson for years, so shouldn't I feel like this is all kinds of wrong?

I know I shouldn't be moving this fast.

I need to slow things down.

But oh my God, the sex was so good.

Fuck.

On the drive home, I am constantly in my head. The visions of August fucking me won't leave me. After what feels like only a few seconds, I arrive home and pull into the driveway, jump out of my car, and run inside.

"Rylee."

I pause at my sister's voice.

I didn't even notice she was there when I stepped into our apartment.

She looks me up and down and the tips of her lips turn up into a wide grin. "Where have you been?" She wiggles her eyebrows as if she already knows the answer to the question.

"I need to sleep," I reply, totally ignoring her question.

"I think I know who made you so tired. Oh, by the way, your Indian came. I guess you got so busy, you forgot about it." She yells the last part as I walk into my room, shutting the door.

Rhianna has a larger room, but that doesn't faze me. Living here means everything to me. I can do whatever I want whenever I want and not worry about coming home late or being concerned I may wake my parents.

I'm not sure why I waited so long to move out. It seems I needed a wake-up call, and Anderson has supplied that in bucketloads. I simply had to build the strength to displease my parents without having that fact weigh on my conscience too heavily.

Working in the family business makes this all the harder, but I had to build the fortitude and simply go for it. Now, I breathe easier, knowing I don't have to deal with their disapproval and criticism of absolutely everything I do. Sure, I hear it at work, but at least I get a breather when I'm home. Living with Rhianna has so many perks, and I finally feel free—free from my parents and free from Anderson—free to live my life any way I want. And the feeling of freedom is so liberating.

"Beckham called. He's coming to spend the day with you tomorrow." She bangs on my door as I close my eyes.

He's been away for the last week at camp, and now he's back. I'm guessing because I'm not home, he needs to discuss what happened.

I love my brother.

When Rhianna moved out, Beckham and I grew closer.

He trusts me with the secrets he doesn't tell anyone, and I appreciate him and help where I can.

My phone dings next to me, and when I go to reach for it, I see Anderson's name flash across the screen.

Goddammit! I turn it off because I do not need him ruining a perfectly good night.

Instead, I go to sleep with dreams of August.

"Wake up." Banging on my door rouses me from sleep. I somehow manage to slide out of bed and pull it open to see Beckham standing on the other side, dressed in his football jersey and some jeans. I let him in, and we walk back to my bedroom and lie on my bed.

"Mom asked about you today. Asked if I could see you, which she already knew I was going to, and that if you could give her the courtesy of coming home to arrange dinners."

"Rhianna only has to do one," I tell him.

"Rhianna isn't the golden child."

"I heard that," Rhianna yells out from her room.

"Like it's something you didn't already know," Beckham yells back. Then he turns around to me. His face is bruised, and his lip is split. I reach out to touch it, but he shakes his head.

"What happened?"

"Nothing," he says, defensively.

"Beckham."

"Anderson has been telling people things about you."

"Of course he has. It's his M.O. to do that shit. You need to ignore him."

"He said that you prefer trailer trash over him." I harumph at his words. "August is better than him anyway, and I don't even know the dude."

"He is better," I say. "But don't fight over it or me. Leave Anderson to run his mouth, it doesn't affect me."

Beckham scratches his head. "You know then?"

"Yes, I know he knocked some skank up."

He sits on my bed next to me. "Actually, she's nice. Jacinta's her name. She stopped me last week and asked about you. Asked for your number, but I didn't give it to her."

"Good. I want nothing to do with either of them. I don't know her, and I don't want to," I tell him. "Beckham, please... stay away from

Anderson and everything that goes with that man."

He takes his baseball cap off his head and shakes his hair out. "Mom is mad... you know... that you called it off with him."

"She can stay mad. I don't care."

"You do care, though. You aren't like Rhianna," he points out.

Beckham is right, but maybe if I tell myself enough times that I don't care, it'll be true.

Probably not, though.

Beckham's phone starts ringing. He answers it, and I overhear my mother's voice on the other end.

"Tell your sister to come for dinner, please. I need to talk to her." Beckham looks at me helplessly, raising his eyebrows, and I take the phone from his hand.

"I have to catch up on work tonight, Mom."

"It's just for a bit. Come on... you have to eat. Don't be silly, Rylee. I'll see you at six." She hangs up, and I pass the phone back to Beckham.

"Do you want me to tell Rhi?" he asks. Knowing full well she'll come and be the bouncer I need between our mother and me.

"No, it's fine. Now, what do you want to do today?" I ask with a genuine smile.

"Go-karting."

"Go-karting it is," I say, standing and pulling on my joggers.

"You came," my mother states as if she knew I wouldn't come as we walk inside.

Beckham goes straight past her and up the stairs to his bedroom.

We had a good day. I needed it, and I think he did too.

"You asked me, did you not?"

She nods and steps off to the kitchen, so I follow her. When we get there, I see Anderson's parents sitting at the table with Anderson as well.

Oh, fuck no.

No. *No*. NO, I scream in my head.

Really? I glare at my mother, who's grinning like she's won some sort of competition as she pulls out a chair for me to sit on. I check around for my father but don't spot him anywhere.

"I must have come at the wrong time," I say

to my mother with a forced smile. "I see you have company. I'll come back another time." I go to leave, but Anderson's mother calls out to me, "Don't be silly, Rylee. Sit, we have things to discuss."

With a sideways glance, I glare at my mother, and if looks could kill, she would positively, absolutely, unequivocally be dead.

"Come, sit." Mom nods for me to sit in the chair she pulled out like my reaction meant nothing to her. I'm dressed in jeans and a shirt that has Tupac printing on it.

Anderson's mother lifts her nose in disgust, I'm assuming at what I am wearing, as I stroll past her.

When I do finally sit, my mother takes the seat next to me and taps her long, fake nails on the table. "So, I have been informed of the issue at hand."

Issue!

Issue?

As if what's happening is an *issue*.

It's a baby.

"Yes, we've been out of our mind with worry," Anderson's mother says with a shake of her head. Everything about this woman is fake—face, eyes, tits, ass—I'm sure she keeps her plastic surgeon in Ferraris.

Anderson's father stays silent, and when I chance a peek at Anderson, his eyes are like liquid heat. Is he angry?

"I can see no problem," I reply with a snarky grin that should let them know just how sarcastic that comment was.

Both sets of mothers' eyes fall to me.

"How can you say that?" my mother asks with a shake of her head. The disappointment is apparent in her eyes. "The man you are going to marry has a massive issue he needs to deal with. Now is the time for you to show your support and be by his side."

"No," I say with a smile, then look at Anderson. "You slept around. You cheated on me. It's your baby. We all know it. So grow up and be a father, and stop letting your mother handle your problems."

The bastard has the audacity to clench his fists on the table while his mother gasps at my words.

He wants to harm me.

I know he does.

But he can't because there are too many people around.

Asshole.

"How dare you! You are meant to be his fiancée," his mother says, nodding to the box sitting in the middle of the table.

The sight of it causes a shiver to run through my body that feels as if someone has just walked over my grave. It's not a good feeling, rather one that makes me want to run and never turn back, so I say while glaring at Anderson, "That's a hard pass."

He stands, slams his fist on the table, and leans forward. "You don't get a say in this. You *will* be my wife."

"Nope. I think not," I say, trying hard to keep my composure.

Anderson moves, pushes his chair out, which falls backward and slams onto the floor, then he rushes around the table. Before he can reach me, his father stands and steps out so he's in front of him, blocking his path. He places a hand on his chest, and Anderson huffs with pinched eyebrows, so much so, they are almost a monobrow, but even more intimidating are his clenched teeth.

He's angry.

No, he's furious.

And if it wasn't for his father, I'm sure I would be laid out on the floor right now.

"You need to leave," Anderson's father says to him, then he turns to me. "You would've been a great asset to our family, Rylee. I'm sorry it didn't work out. Anderson will *not* bother you again." His father drops his hand from his son's chest and holds his hand out for his wife, who clearly wants to say more but holds her tongue. She stands, and they all hurry out, leaving me sitting with my mother at the table.

"How dare you. Are you trying to be like your sister?" my mother shrieks, her hands waving around like she's some sort of madwoman. She reaches for the ring that was left on the table and opens the box.

It's beautiful. The pink diamond is massive, but it's not something I would choose. However, I cannot deny how stunning it is if you're into ostentatious shows of wealth.

"You could have had this. Had so much." She turns to face me. "Why would you ruin it?"

"He isn't right for me," I tell her. "We haven't been right for each other for a long time. Mom, he cheated. He is going to have a damn baby with someone else. What part of that makes you think he could possibly be right for me?"

My father walks in and kisses the top of my head. "I couldn't agree more," he says, having heard what I said. My mother pins him with her death stare as I get up.

"I have to go. Work tomorrow," I say, leaning down and kissing my mother's cheek, followed by my father's.

"You can still change your mind," my mother calls out to me.

I don't answer.

Because that is not happening.

Hell hasn't frozen over the last time I looked.

CHAPTER 14

To say I haven't woken up without my cock rock fucking hard since I last had Rylee would be an understatement.

Rich girl hasn't called.

Rich girl hasn't visited.

And for some reason, I like that about her.

I'm sitting at the front of the house waiting for Paige to finish school. Today's the day she's meant to come over, and she has been hounding me to get fresh pastry, and the other ingredients so she can make quiches.

However, I am unsettled as it's getting late and she isn't here.

Standing back up and going inside, I reach for my phone and call her. When the phone picks up, my heart almost stops.

"August boy, what you doing, my man?"

I pull the phone away from my ear to make sure I dialed the right number, and sure enough, I know it's correct.

"Why the fuck do you have my sister's phone?"

"Oh, come on, August... you know why. I fuck your mother." He cackles.

That cackle makes me want to throw something, or better yet, break his damn jaw.

"Hey, look... I need you to do something for me."

"No," I reply while sliding on my shoes.

"Come on, August, just like old times. I need a favor, and, well... Paige isn't in the mood to do it right now."

"What do you mean... *isn't in the mood?*"

"Like mother, like daughter. You should know this. Are you really that blind?"

"Where is she?"

"I told you, I need you first," he says again. I hear a giggle in the background and close my front door.

"Go to Alfred's and collect for me. You know what to do. You haven't forgotten." He hangs up, and I resist the urge to throw my phone, to smash it into a million pieces.

Alfred is a local dealer who usually owes Josh a lot of money. Back then, with all the other stupid jobs I did for Josh, he would make me collect from him. Sometimes beat his clients up and take whatever they had on them.

Last time, it was his car.

I start running, arriving at Alfred's place as quickly as I can. When I get to the front of the house, I don't bother to knock, simply kick open the door and find Alfred by himself, sitting on the floor with his merch in front of him.

This is why he always owes money, because he uses it.

His hollow eyes blink a few times and glance up to find me standing in his living room. It takes him a second to realize it's me before he starts scooting backward on his ass, spilling product all over himself and the floor.

"You're back." His voice croaks as he speaks.

"Where's the payment, Alfred? I have to go."

He looks over to his television and nods. I rush over and open the black box sitting in front of the unit. Yanking up the lid, I see the cash.

"He set you up, you know. Why are you back with him?"

"I'm not," I reply before heading out, box in hand, leaving him to get high all by him fucking self.

I only have one job, protecting my sister, she's all that matters right now.

Josh is sitting out the front when I march to him. He has a cigarette in one hand and a glass of alcohol in the other. His eyes fall to the black box in my hand, then to me, and he shows me his rotten teeth in some sort of sneer.

"I knew you could do it," he says, then nods to the money. "Take half as your payment."

I throw the entire box at him, and he moves just in time for it to miss smashing into his useless head. Josh doesn't live in the dumps like most drug pushers. No. The man isn't stupid and doesn't smoke nor use his product, but he does prefer the same drug as my mother, alcohol.

"Paige," I yell.

The front door opens. Even though it's a fucking mess inside, the outside has you fooled. Appearances make it look like it's owned by someone who cares. Not someone who doesn't give two shits about anyone or anything but himself.

When I see my mother standing there, I shake my head. "Where's Paige?"

"August, come now... have a drink."

I turn to stare at him. My hands are in clenched fists. He taps his side, where I know he keeps his gun. It's what he uses to threaten those who don't listen to him, and the problem is I know he can use it.

"Fuck off. I did what you asked, now give her to me." That's when I see Paige. She steps up behind our mother and leans on the wall for support.

Fuck.

Fuck.

Walking straight over to her, I grab her face and check her eyes, then her arms.

"You drunk?" I ask. She nods, but the smile she gives me doesn't reach her eyes. "Come on, you shouldn't be around this trash."

"Hey, I'm your mother."

"You're not a mother's asshole," I spit to her. "Paige, start walking." I reach for her as and she steps out of the house and smells like cigarette smoke. Her father is going to whip her ass and then mine.

Has she been doing this for long?

"I wonder if I can get you to do more things for her," Josh says, looking at Paige. "I never thought I would see the day that you care for someone other than yourself, August boy." He pauses, thinking about something. "What about that other girl I saw you with last week? We all know who she is."

It's no secret. Everyone knows who they are. Their family is one of the richest in our town.

Ignoring Josh because I know all he wants is a reaction from me, I keep walking, practically dragging Paige behind me.

I need a fucking car.

About halfway home, she stops and leans over, spewing. She misses my shoes by a fraction and I jump back.

"Fuck, Paige. How the fuck am I going to explain this to your father?"

She starts shaking her head. Then continues to be physically ill. When I think she's finished, I pick her up and throw her over my shoulder.

She hangs on, barely, as I run the rest of the way home.

When I finally step inside, I place her on the couch and grab a bucket, putting it next to her, then go to my phone and call her father.

He answers straight away. "August, everything okay?"

"Paige is here," I tell him.

"Oh, she was meant to be staying at Courtney's tonight." He pauses. "I'll come get her."

"Look..." I scratch the back of my neck. "There's something you should know."

"August..."

"I found her at Carina's," I tell him, using my mother's name.

"Is she okay?"

"She's drunk."

He pauses again, and I hear him saying something to someone else, followed by silence before he talks again. "You aren't allowed to interact with Josh, August. How did you get her?" he asks with suspicion.

He thinks I'm back with him.

I don't blame him.

I protected him, beat people for him, and sold for him.

But it was for money.

I needed to survive, and that was my survival.

At the time, I had no other options. No one in this town would hire someone like me.

"I had to do a job to get her," I tell him, and I don't know why I do. "I'm not working for him. It was his condition for me being allowed to collect her."

"Of course it was. He wants you back. His clients are all scared of you. He needs that fear... he doesn't have that bargaining chip anymore." He huffs. "I'm almost there." He hangs up, and I head over to Paige and push her hair back as she starts throwing up again.

My front door opens, and Glenn walks in, straight to Paige, complete in his police uniform.

"How long has she been seeing her?" I ask Glenn.

"She hadn't been... well, as far as I was aware," he replies and reaches down for her. She opens her eyes and scoots back on the couch. "Paige, you're coming home." He helps her sit up, and when she does, she looks back at me with hard eyes.

"Don't go to that house again," I tell her.

"You shouldn't have called him," she says, as a tear falls from her eye.

"I had to."

"Yes, he did," Glenn says and nods to me as he strolls out with Paige in his arms.

CHAPTER 15

"When was the last time you saw him?" Rhianna asks as we drive to our parents' house the following weekend. It's been a week since I sat there in front of Anderson and his parents and even longer since I've seen August.

One man I couldn't care less for, the other, well, he visits me in my dreams.

"That night when you saw us," I tell her, pulling into the driveway.

"Well, Noah told me something interesting about him." She closes the door, and we walk to the front.

"What?"

"You know all that furniture in his house? Noah said you had seen it." I nod, and we wait before opening the front door. "He makes it all. Noah said he's now making it for some of his top clients after he made a desk for Noah's office as a thank you." I don't say anything, just nod. "He's good. Noah said the desk he made is probably one of the best he's ever seen."

Our mother opens the door and says, "Why are you waiting out here?"

"Ry was telling me all about work. You know, that fun place she goes to every day." Rhianna walks past our mother, whose eyes fall on me.

"Where is Noah?" our mother asks, her eyes staying on me, but she's asking Rhianna.

"Working," she says and calls me. "Ry, come on, what are you doing?"

"Anderson is here," my mother says quietly.

I sigh. Really?

Oh my God, what part of no does she not understand.

I go to step back only to hear my sister yell, "What the fuck are *you* doing here?"

Our mother immediately leaves me and hurries to Rhi. I follow and see Rhianna's arms crossed over each other, pushing her breasts up as she stares at him.

Anderson stands, and his eyes fall to me. "I want to talk to you." His voice is kind, and I know better than to fall for that bullshit.

"Nope, not happening," Rhianna states.

"Rhianna, stay out of it," our mother chides.

Rhianna's mouth opens in astonishment.

"Maybe you should take your own advice. I heard what you did last week." Rhianna points at her, then turns back to Anderson. "*You… you* need to leave. Stop being so damn desperate. She's moved on, for God's sake. She doesn't want your cheating ass anymore."

I cringe at her words because she just told him I've moved on.

When I check, I can tell that's all he heard as well. His eyes narrow and he goes to take a step toward me, but Rhi blocks his path and sets herself so he can't get to me.

"*Leave*, Anderson," she says again.

"Maybe today is not a good time," our mother finally says. "We can organize another time."

Anderson starts to leave, but before he does, as he walks past me, he reaches for my arm, catches it, and leans in. "We need to talk."

I pull my arm free. "No, we don't." I step back so he can't reach for me again.

His eyes fly to my sister, then back to me,

before he spins on his heels and leaves.

After he's gone, I turn to my mother. "If you do that again, I won't be back," I tell her.

"How could you do that? Do you not care at all about Rylee's feelings?" Rhianna says, coming to my defense as always. "She doesn't love him. So why would you want her to be with someone who cheats on her?"

"Sometimes love is a sacrifice." She straightens her shoulders.

"No, you meant to say love is money," Rhianna chimes in.

Our father strolls in with Beckham next to him. I forgot how much they look alike with their dark hair and gray eyes.

"What's going on?" our father asks. We both stand there waiting for Mom to say something, but she simply offers a smile, says nothing as she walks to the kitchen. Our father follows, leaving us standing there with Beckham.

"What happened?"

"Don't worry about it," Rhi says at the same time I say, "Anderson was here."

Rhi's eyes go wide.

I shrug.

"And let me guess, she let him in," he says, nodding in the direction our mother went.

"Yep."

"You should go," he says.

Rhi nods in agreement.

"She shouldn't have done that, and if you keep letting her get away with that shit, she will continue to do it." Rhianna places a hand on my shoulder. "Go... visit a friend." She winks.

"What friend?" Beckham asks.

This time, I don't tell him. "No one." He scrunches up his nose and shakes his head before he heads off.

"How are you going to get home?" I ask Rhi because I drove here.

"I'll just text my booty call," she replies. "He'll come to get me. Don't worry. Make your escape and go see *your* booty call."

"Yeah, that's a no," I declare, stepping toward the door.

When I turn back, Rhi is on her phone, texting Noah.

"How have we completely changed positions? I would never leave an event with Mom or Dad. You, on the other hand, I covered for millions of times."

Rhi puts her phone in her purse and heads over to kiss my cheek. "You've stopped drinking the poison and finally seen the light." She pushes me out the door and shuts it firmly behind me.

I blink a few times at the shut door, then spin on my heel and get the hell out of there.

I don't call August or even go to his place. Even though I would love to have another taste of him. Instead, I go to the bar. A few of my work colleagues are having drinks, and usually, I turn them down. Being the owner's daughter of the business that, one day, will be mine—which I might add isn't forced because I love what I do— I've never interacted outside of business with any of the employees because my father never does.

I spot Shandy first. She is also an accountant. She takes on the small-scale business clientele while only a few of us handle the larger accounts, my father and I handling the biggest. She turns, and her fiery red hair swings when she does. Shandy is one of the only people in the office who's my age.

"Rylee, you made it. Holy shit." She pulls me in for a one-arm hug, "What's your poison? I'm a gin girl, myself."

"I'll have the same."

"Awesome." I stand behind her as she orders, and when she's finished with the bartender, she turns straight back to me. "I never thought you'd actually come, but I always invite you just in case you change your mind. I'm so happy you're here."

My cheeks start to heat as I pull my handbag up higher on my shoulder. "Thanks. Yeah, I had no plans this evening... so thought, why not." She smiles and hands me my drink and nods over to where there are a few of the other staff sitting around a table.

"Come... they're in big talks about paranormal right now. Do *not* even ask me how we got onto this subject." She laughs as she takes a seat and nods for me to sit next to her.

"Rylee, wow! Didn't expect to see you here," Benji says next to me.

I give him a small gracious smile and bring my drink to my lips.

"Hey, aren't you usually always with your boyfriend?" Harrison asks. This is a man who should really be at home with his wife. A man who, if I remember correctly, has just had a baby.

"How's your wife?" I ask.

Someone laughs, and I turn to Shandy.

"Werewolves don't actually turn into wolves," one of them says, going back to their conversation. "And vampires don't actually fly."

Benji leans forward, his face serious. "They do fly if they are old enough. And, of course, they turn into wolves. It's where they got the name. Come on, what planet are you living on?"

I listen, sipping my drink, quietly thinking

what the hell are they discussing, when someone taps me on my shoulder. Spinning around to a man I don't recognize at all, I can't help but narrow my eyes.

"Hey, you're August's friend, right?"

Okay, that's weird.

"No," I answer, then turn away to gather my thoughts. Shandy is watching the dude intently, and I notice a slight head shake, which I have no idea what that means.

"How about a drink?" he asks.

"She said no," Shandy replies for me, her lips are thinned as she glares.

I glance around the table—the others are not paying any attention as they fight about werewolves.

"I only want to talk. No beef, lady." When I turn around to him again, he's studying me. "It's nice to meet you, Rylee. I'm Josh. Tell August I said hi." He winks and then walks out of the bar.

Umm, okay.

"That was weird. Did you know him?" Shandy asks, her eyes firmly set on the exit.

"No. Not at all."

"He probably recognized you from somewhere. I bet you get that a lot." She taps her glass to mine and turns back to the conversation.

Okay, is that strange too?

I reach for my phone and message August.

Someone said to say hi. Josh... do you know
him?

I wait, and when he doesn't respond, I put my phone on my lap and join in the conversation. Shandy's nice, and she starts discussing her private life. She lives by herself, and her family has a house in a different state, so everyone she's met has been from work, as she moved specifically for the job.

My phone beeps in my lap as we stand to get a second drink, and I glance down, reading the message.

Where are you?

No hello, nothing.

So I choose to ignore it and step off to the bar. I shout a round of drinks for the table, and when I return, there are a few missed calls.

I'm at Wobbly.

I text back, choosing not to call him. I'm not sure I want to hear his voice right now. Dreams of him are enough without having to hear him as well.

"So you and your boyfriend... it's a no-go?" Shandy asks quietly.

"Separated."

She nods. "You okay?"

"Yeah, it was time. We passed our expiration date a long time ago."

"Can I say something you may not like to hear?" She bites her lip.

"Umm... sure."

"He tried to hit on me every time he came in. Honestly, it gave me the heebie-jeebies." She shivers.

Of course he did.

"Don't look now, but... holy shit! The most devastatingly gorgeous man has just walked in, and well, crap... he's coming this way." She sits taller and pushes her tits up, which are already spilling out of the top of her dress. I have to laugh until that gorgeous man is standing directly in front of my chair.

As I glance up from the floor, I see black boots, followed by black jeans, a green shirt encasing steel-hard shoulders, and a tense jaw as he stares down at me.

Oh, shit! Is he pissed?

Forest green eyes lock on to mine. "We need to talk," he says, and it seems everyone stops their conversation.

I stand and nod at Shandy. "I'll just be a minute." Turning and heading for the door, I feel him behind me every step of the way until the cold air hits my face and sends a shiver over my entire body. When I turn around to ask him if everything is all right, he's pacing back and forth with his hands bunched into tight fists by his sides. But even more concerning are the flared nostrils and the noisy breathing through his nose. He sounds like a raging bull.

"Where is he?"

"Huh?" I ask with a grimace.

"Josh. Was he here?"

Oh, that. I nod, to which he steps closer until our chests are almost touching.

"Stay away from him. If he comes near you, you will walk the other way."

"You couldn't have texted that tidbit of information?" I ask, scrunching my brows in confusion.

"He's dangerous. Stay away."

I nod. I mean, what else can I do, but this makes him grind his teeth.

I've had a few drinks, and I was happy. I should be worried, but instead, I'm turned on.

"Want to come in for a drink?" I ask, nodding my head to the bar.

He glances that way, then back to me, his eyes raking me up and down before he nods.

I am *so* getting lucky tonight.

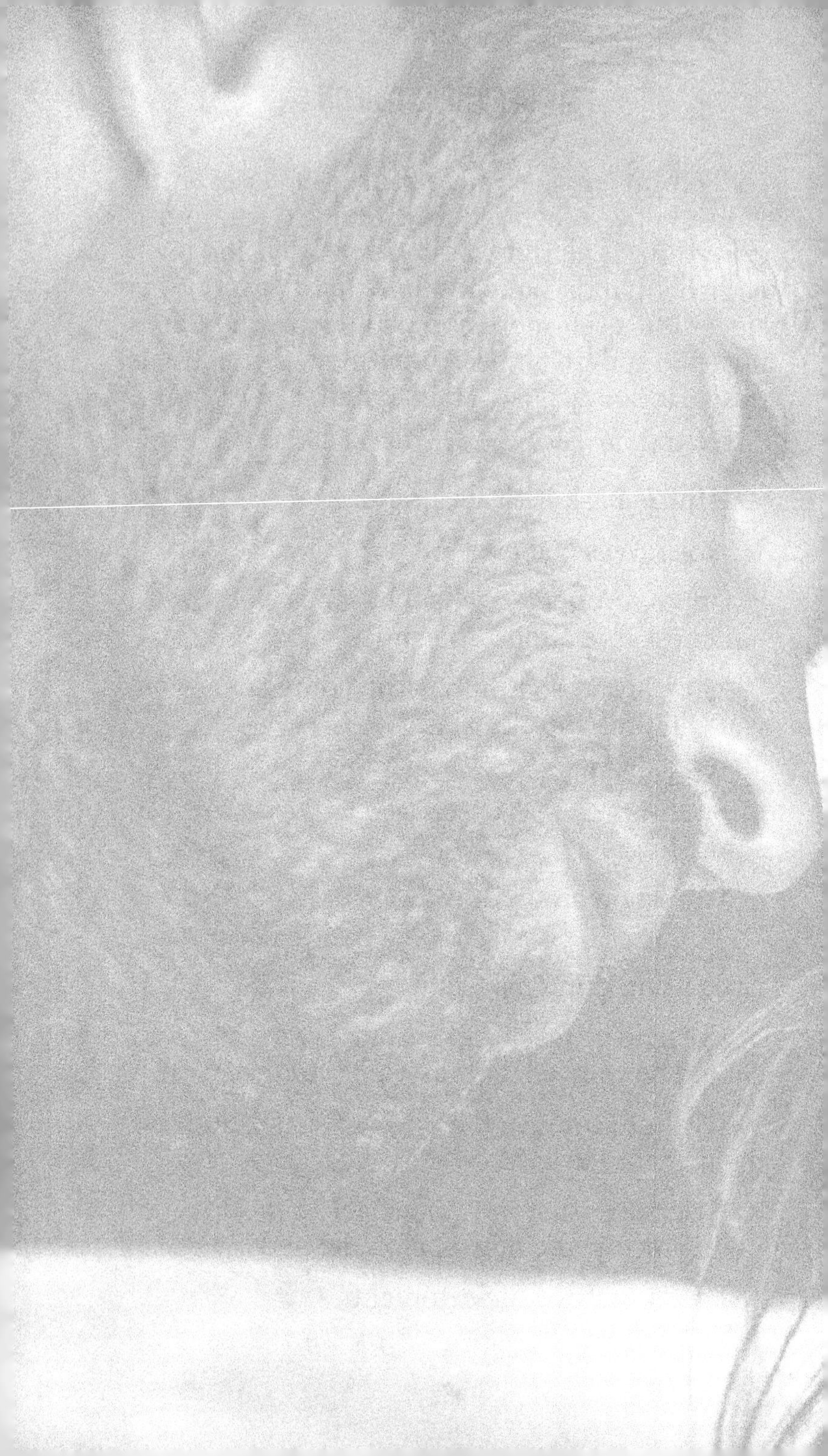

CHAPTER 16

August

Probably against my better judgment, I follow Rylee inside the bar. She's wearing a tight, pink dress that hugs her perfect ass, with white heels accentuating her legs that I can imagine wrapped around my neck. Those shoes are probably the only reason I agreed to come in.

Because I hate people.

For some reason, though, little Miss Rylee Harley seems to have the opposite effect on me.

I don't dislike her, even though I've tried to stay away.

Believe me, I've tried.

Her friend with the red hair checks me out and then grins.

Rylee reaches for my hand and pulls me down to sit next to her.

"Shandy, this is August," Rylee introduces us.

"Nice to meet you," she replies.

Rylee puts her drink to her lips, and I want to taste them so badly right now.

"You want one?" Rylee asks before placing the glass on the table.

"No. I'll drive."

She nods, which makes Shandy lean in close to Rylee. They think they're whispering, but they aren't, and I can hear every goddamn word.

"Is this your new flavor? Because he's way better than that other asshole. He won't even look at me. That man only has eyes for you."

I try not to smirk at her words.

"He's my new dessert. Yes." She smiles, and then she winks at me before picking her glass up again and finishes off her drink.

"Hey, you're not Anderson. Who are you?" a guy who's clearly older than me turns and says.

Rylee answers before I can, "None of your business, Benji. Shouldn't you be at home already?"

"If you weren't the boss's daughter," he says, shaking his head and lifting his beer to his mouth to obviously stop what he was about to say.

"Yeah, you would what?" she fires back, her elbows lean on her bare knees.

I want to pull her back before his eyes fall to her cleavage—that pair of tits are hard not to stare at.

"Never mind," he mumbles.

Rylee drops a hand on my knee, turns back to her friend, and starts talking. Her hand begins to slide up my leg, and I have to place my hand on top of hers to stop it. Giving it a squeeze, she chuckles.

"I'm getting a bit tired. Do you want to go?" Rylee asks, her voice dropping down to a sexy whisper.

"You're drunk."

"I like sex when I'm drunk," she says louder than she intended, making everyone's eyes fixate on us.

I stand and reach for her purse, then guide her outside.

She giggles as we head out, then she grips my ass in her hand, giving it a firm squeeze. "I've always wanted to do that," she says, then leans on me.

"Always?"

"Yes. From the first day I saw you walking the halls of our school."

I stop and lift her chin with my finger. "You've wanted me since high school?"

Her eyelashes flutter before she licks her lips. My eyes drop straight to them. They're pinker than usual tonight, and I wonder what they taste like again.

"Every girl wanted you." She's breathing quite heavily, then she steps forward, putting no distance between us, our bodies touching. "And now, I have you."

Wrong. Oh, so wrong.

I step back and unlock her car, opening her door so she can slide in. She's confused, I can tell by the tilt of her head, but she soon shakes it off.

Driving her back to her place, she stares at me the whole drive but doesn't say a word until we arrive.

"You should come in. Stay."

"No. I have work to do."

"Come." Her hand slides over my jeans and onto my cock. "I'll make it worth your while." I glance at her hand and then back to her dark soulless eyes. They're glassy tonight.

"No. Do you need me to walk you inside?"

She pulls her hand away like it's on fire. "No! I know how to get in."

I stay seated in her car. Pointing to the keys, I ask, "Which key do you need? I'll bring the car back in the morning."

She nods to the right one then gets out.

When she reaches the door, I wait for her to step inside. Her eyes find mine, and I don't leave until the door is shut.

"She's still asleep," Noah says, opening the door to Rylee's apartment the next day. I hand him the keys. "You took her car?"

"She was drunk."

He nods in understanding. "Look, it's not my place, but with what's going on, you two seem to be spending plenty of time together." He has a firm grip on his coffee.

"You're right. It's not your place." He nods and accepts my answer. I like Noah. He's treated me with more respect than most people have my entire life.

But this part of my life—what I have with Rylee—I don't share with anyone. Because let's face it, even I don't know what it is yet.

How can it even be anything?

She's a rich girl wanting to fuck a bad boy.

The problem—it's explained as easily as that.

My problem—I let her because her rich girl pussy is fucking dynamite.

Explosive.

Like a fucking deer caught in the headlights.

And I can't seem to walk away.

"Do you need a lift back home?" Noah asks.

I rub the back of my head. "Actually, I need a favor."

"Yeah?"

"Can I borrow a truck? I need to get wood."

Noah doesn't say anything. He simply walks away, then comes back with his keys in hand. "It's new, don't fucking ruin it," he states as he passes them to me.

"Thanks, man, I appreciate it."

Noah nods his head and turns to shut the door.

Quick stepping it to his truck, I hear my name called, "August." Turning, I see Rylee standing there, her dark hair stuck to her face, but she's still dressed in the same stunning pink dress she was wearing last night.

"I want to apologize... for last night."

"Why?" I ask, pulling open the door to the truck.

Rylee frowns, confusion written on her face, and then she shakes her head. "For all of it."

"You don't remember, do you?"

Her eyebrows pinch. "I do. Most of it anyway."

I laugh and climb into the truck.

"Where are you going?"

"To get supplies."

"Can I come?" My brows pull together when I stare at what she's wearing and don't reply. "I'll get changed. Just… can you wait a few minutes?" She runs off without allowing me to give her an answer.

I check the dash for the time and think I will wait exactly five minutes. If she's not back by then, I'm leaving. But that's when I see her running out, pulling a shirt over her head. She pulls on the passenger side door and throws her bag on the backseat before she climbs in. She's obviously showered—quickest damn shower on record—because she smells amazing, and she's thrown her hair up in a bun on top of her head.

"You showered?" I ask because I am impressed.

Rylee lifts her pelvis forward and does up the top button of her shorts before she sits back down and pulls the seat belt across her body.

"Quickly, but yes. I stank."

With one shake of my head, I pull the truck out.

When we hit the road, she leans over and takes my sunglasses from the top of my head. "My eyes are hurting." She puts them on her face and then glances over to me. "So, where are we going?"

"It's Sunday. I'm sure you have more important things to do than what I'm going to be doing."

"Nope, no plans." She smiles. "I'm all yours."

"Great," I murmur under my breath, the sarcasm is not hidden, but she hears me anyway.

"We should get to know each other," she declares when the silence gets too much for her.

"Why?"

"Because we could be friends."

"Yeah, that *won't* happen," I argue back.

"Why, because I'm a girl?"

"No, because I've fucked your pussy."

Taking a sharp left, I turn into the landscaping place to pick up supplies.

"You should try it. From what I see... you don't seem to have any friends, besides maybe Noah. And I want to be one to you."

"Again, we've fucked. People who fuck can't be friends."

"No more fucking then. Forget it happened."

"You want to forget we fucked?" I ask, and

cannot help the giant smirk that forms on my face.

She shakes her head. "Yes, it's already forgotten. Now... friends?" she asks, holding out her hand for me to shake.

I blink once, sigh and glance down at it, then turn and to get out of the truck—I'm not shaking on that. Striding around to her side, I open the door and offer her my hand. She takes it as she slides out, and when she does, I make sure to press my body against hers, which makes her breath hitch and her bottom lip quiver. I lean in close, lifting the sunglasses away from her face to see her eyes already trained in on my lips.

Just when she thinks I'm about to kiss her, I pull back. "See... you still want to fuck me." I release her and leave her standing there.

"That's unfair. I'm on damn fire here, and you need to put out the flames," she yells from behind me.

I stop in my tracks. Everyone in the yard looks our way. I can't fight the upturn of my lips when I turn back to see her climbing back into the truck, embarrassed by her outburst.

Friends.

What a joke.

Because I plan to fuck her nine ways to Sunday.

CHAPTER 17

Rylee

I sit in the truck for ages waiting for him—I'm hungry, thirsty, and want sex. When August finally returns, he loads up the back of the truck with all his purchases before he gets in. He's covered in sweat, then he spins his head around and asks, "Feel better?" His lips pull up.

I want to smack that smirk right off his face, but he throws me a drink, and I take it with eager hands.

"No, I'm hungry..." I pause, not wanting to embarrass myself any further. "Thank you."

"I'll cook you something when we get home. You think Noah will bring your car over to mine so we can swap back?"

I nod, knowing he will.

Shooting Noah a quick message, he replies straight away.

"He said he'll be at yours in a few hours."

"You and your sister are quite different for identical twins." His hand grips the wheel tightly as he starts talking to me.

"Of course we are. We don't share the same brain," I reply. We always get comments and questions like that. Things like...

Are you alike?

Why does she do that, and you don't? Aren't you identical?

It's the same thing over and over.

My favorite one from guys is...

Two for the price of one. My dreams are coming true.

Yeah, can you say eww?

"What's it like, having a twin?"

Surprisingly, no one has asked me that question before, and it's a pleasant change.

"Growing up it was good. We didn't really know who we were back then, so it was all a giant learning curve. We could trick our mother, but never Beckham. He was the only one we could never fool with our antics…" I pause, smiling. "When we reached sixteen… that was when we realized we're nothing alike. Not even down to our favorite colors. And especially not our taste in men. But we always stuck together. She's literally the only person I know I would tell if I killed someone, and her first response would be, 'So, what do we do with the body?'" I sigh.

"Must be nice to have someone like that to confide in," he says, pulling into his driveway.

"I'd help you hide a body, August. That is… if we were friends." I wink at him, getting out of the truck.

I hear his laughter as we both stroll around to the back of the truck. He starts to unload, and I grab the smaller pieces that I can carry and leave all the larger ones for him. We don't talk as we work, but I can feel his eyes on me. Just as we're finishing, Noah pulls up with my sister in tow. She slides out of the car and heads straight over and throws her arm through mine.

"You're dirty. And not in a good way either."

"Girls, we can hear you," Noah says, smiling widely at Rhianna.

"Hush you." She turns back to me. "Dinner tonight? If you don't have any other plans, that is?"

August, who has his shirt off, is wiping his face with it.

"I mean, I would give me a pass if I was looking at that," Rhianna states.

"Can still hear you," Noah reminds her.

August's eyes find mine and quickly shift away as he goes back to emptying the truck.

"Sure, I'll see you then."

She and Noah take off, leaving me alone again with August. I follow him out the back of his home to the shed where all the wood is piled, and watch as he opens the big double doors. Inside are tools hanging on the wall, which I have no idea what they're for, and a large bench running down the middle. "You make all your things here?" I question, stepping in through the doors. Down at the very end of the garage is a large table that holds a few of his works in progress. I run my hand over the smooth wood and turn back to him.

"Woodworking was the only class I enjoyed," he tells me, referring back to his high school days. "Then, in prison, it was the same. It kept me occupied and helped to pass the time." He shrugs. "I like to make things with my hands."

"Will you make me something?" I ask. "I'll pay you, of course."

"What could you possibly need?"

"Surprise me," I reply.

August wipes his hands on the shirt, which he tucked into the top of his jeans and is now hanging down the side of his leg. He starts to head back to the house. "Come on, I'm starving."

I follow him inside and to the kitchen, where he starts pulling out food from the refrigerator and then pours himself a glass of milk. When he offers me a glass, I shake my head, scrunching up my nose.

Milk on its own is disgusting.

How he can drink it like that? I have no idea.

A knock on the door is heard, and he places the glass down, stepping off to answer it. I can't see who it is, but I can definitely hear them.

"August, look... I know you did the right thing..." The visitor pauses. "She's been asking to see you." I step into view so whoever it is knows I'm here. Officer Glenn is standing at the front door with Paige by his side. He scrunches his eyes in confusion as he checks between us.

"Miss Harley," he says, nodding to me.

"Hi, Glenn, Paige, good to see you both."

"Am I interrupting anything?" Glenn asks.

"No, Rylee was helping me carry the wood out back."

Glenn nods. "Okay, well, anyway... like I said,

Paige has been asking for you. I figure she's in safe hands here."

August nods and steps aside, letting Paige in. She marches past me at speed and straight to the kitchen.

"Don't let her go anywhere, and thank you again for last time."

August nods before Glenn gives me one last glance as he leaves. When he shuts the door, August turns to me.

"Should I go?" I ask.

"No. Stay," he says, and I can't fight the smile that touches my lips as he returns to the kitchen. August goes straight back to cooking while I sit next to Paige on the two stools he has at his kitchen counter.

"Aren't you even going to look at me?" Paige asks with a hoarse voice, on the verge of tears. "August," she implores, not able to hold back the tears that well in her eyes and slip over, running down her cheeks.

He places the knife on the counter and faces her, then shakes his head before he goes back to cutting.

"August," I chastise.

Paige starts sobbing and gets up, excusing herself before she walks away.

"That girl is clearly upset." He clenches his

jaw at my words but doesn't answer me. "Fine then." I stand and follow Paige, where she has closed herself off in the bathroom. Knocking, I ask, "Can I come in?"

"Yeah." Her voice is low.

When I open the door, she's sitting on the edge of the bathtub, covering her face.

"Hey, don't worry about it. I'm sure everything will be all right." I pat her back, leaning in.

"No, it won't. I knew he would get mad, but I did it anyway."

"Did what?"

Paige lifts her head, and I see the exact same forest-green eyes as August's staring back at me.

"I went and saw her, and when I did, well… she's a drunk, and I guess like mother, like daughter—," she drifts off, wiping at her tears.

"You got drunk with your mom?" I ask, trying to figure it all out in my mind.

"Yes. August hates her. But she's our mother. How can he hate her so much when all she talks about is him?"

"Because she's using that to get to you. Has she asked you yet to start selling? Maybe your body?" August asks, standing in the doorway.

I gape at him, shocked, unable to speak.

"She would never."

"That there... those few words prove to me you don't know who she is. Stay away from them, Paige. I mean it. They're nothing but trouble."

"She loves us."

"No, she doesn't. She loves the idea of using us. That's all that woman will ever care about," he says, then steps inside the small space. "Food is ready."

I nod, getting the message. As I pass by August on my way out, my arm brushes across his.

"You're all she ever talks about," Paige says to August as I walk out the door slowly, trying to listen in to the conversation that I know will now ensue.

"She stopped worrying about if I was bathed or not when I was six. She stopped feeding me when I was ten. She never once visited me in prison. No letter. No nothing. Tell me, Paige, does that sound like all the hallmarks of a doting mother?"

"You sound like Dad," she spits.

"Listen to him. Because..." he pauses for a few seconds then continues, "... he's right."

Wanting to give them some privacy, I go and sit on the front porch. It's then I realize I'm sitting on a wooden chair. The wood, although old in texture, looks brand-new and is sanded to perfection, then stained with something to keep the texture. The legs of the chair are shaped like wooden wheels that sit on a sled-styled bottom. There are two of them with a table in a similar pattern sitting between them.

The chair is unique, stunning, and I love it. The arms seem to have an ornate pattern engraved into the surface, and I can't help but rub my hands back and forward over the surface of the polished wood.

"I'm sure the chair is enjoying the rubbing you're giving it." My hand pauses on the surface of the wood.

"Did you make it?"

August crosses his arms over his chest, making his muscles stand out even more.

"Yes."

"Shouldn't you be covered in tattoos?"

"Why? Because I've been away in prison? Is that why you think I should be covered in ink?" He laughs as Paige finally walks out, her tears now dried. "Come on, rich girl, the food is ready," he says, nodding back to the house.

I can't help but take another look at the chairs.

"August is gifted," Paige says, smiling now. She's obviously proud of her brother's talent. "What's going on with you two?"

My phone starts ringing, and I see Anderson's name flash on the screen. Pressing ignore, I give my attention back to Paige. "Nothing." I stand and pull my keys from my pocket with a smile. "Tell August I said bye. Sorry, I have to go."

She nods and says nothing more as I get in my car to leave.

August walks outside, glancing over at me in the car. My hands freeze on the wheel, but I manage to drive off, even if my head is screaming at me to go back to him.

Pulling over because I'm starving, I stop to grab some food before I go home and sleep for the rest of the day before dinner with Rhi. As I grab a drink, a woman steps in front of me, blocking my view. I attempt to step around her, and it's then I can tell it's the same woman from that night at the party with Anderson. My eyes fall to her belly, which is round. It's not overly large, but it is more than obvious she is pregnant.

"You're Rylee, right?" she asks.

"Yes."

"He told me I wasn't good enough for him. That *we* weren't." She rubs her belly. "He said you were meant to have his babies, no one else."

"I'm not sure what you want me to say," I reply, my eyebrows drawn together.

She shakes her head as if trying to remove the vision from her mind. "I'm sorry, that's all I wanted to say. I didn't know about you when we hooked up. He told me he was single. And when I found out he wasn't, I left. Until..." She looks down at her belly, rubbing it again. "Well... until I found out about the baby. And I knew if he lied to me before, about you, well... he would say this baby wasn't his when I know it is. So I had a DNA test done so he couldn't deny it."

"Umm... okay." I don't know why she feels the need to tell me all this.

"Look... I know this is weird. But I want you to know that I didn't know about you." Tears start to slip from her eyes, falling down her cheeks and dropping onto the front of her dress.

"How old are you?"

She swipes them away, obviously angry she's letting it all get to her. "Eighteen," she replies.

Gosh.

Oh my God, she's closer to my brother's age than Anderson's.

"Just don't—" I cut myself off because I can't tell her what to do. I can't say that one day he might hurt her as well. It's simply not my place to do that. So instead, I say, "Good luck, and no hard feelings." I step around her and give her the best smile I can muster.

Fuck.

Anderson is a real fucking dick.

CHAPTER
18

August

"Are you going to tell me what's going on with you two?" Paige asks while I hand her a glass of milk.

"Eat." She does as I say but continues to stare at me. "Nothing is going on."

"Funny how your answers are the same."

I shake my head.

"I'm sorry, you know. It's hard. I'm a girl, August, surrounded by men. Did you know when I got my first period, Dad had to google what to do?" She shivers. "I wanted a mother to help me. I needed a mother, so I could ask all the questions. Instead, I had to resort to a search on the internet."

"She isn't a mother, and you should know that."

"Yeah, but she's the only one I've got."

I guess it's different for us. I didn't need her back then like Paige needs her now. I won't understand because I'm not a girl, but I'll try to help her if I can.

"You don't need her, Paige. I'm sure you have other girls you can talk to. What about Beckham's mother?"

She coughs and shakes her head. "No, Mrs. Harley is not someone you go to for advice. Rylee, on the other hand..." She smiles up at me. "I'd go to Rylee."

"Hmm..."

"Rylee is good. I like her. Don't you?"

"Hmm..." I turn around and start clearing the mess.

"You can't ignore everything I ask about her, August."

"I'll stop ignoring you if you promise never to go to that house again."

"Josh seems nice," she says defensively.

I turn fast with cloth in hand.

"No. No, he is *not*. Stay far away from him, Paige. Do you understand me?"

"Okay, okay!"

"Tell me you will. If you see him, you'll walk the other way. Promise me."

She rolls her eyes, but I'm not joking. "Paige," I bark her name, making her eyes snap up to mine.

"Yes, okay, I get it."

"Good."

Rylee messages me twice the following week, warning me she is coming over.

Friend.

That's how she ends the messages.

Friend.

My dick twitches at the thought of seeing her. Fuck! What I wouldn't give to throw her over my couch and have her all over again.

What a sweet life that would be.

On Thursday, she rocks up, carrying two bags. Holding the door open for her, she barges in, holding up the bags.

"I ordered us some pizza and dessert. Because people who don't have dessert after a meal are considered evil, just so you know." She struts along, her heels clicking on my wooden floors as she goes, dressed in a knee-length skirt and a white blouse. I can see the outline of her bra through it at the top. It's obviously her work outfit.

"What if I was cooking?"

"Were you?" she bites back. When I don't answer, she starts pulling the food out of the takeout bags. "Thought so. Now... say thank you, and sit down and have a meal with me."

"You're bossy. Is it because you want sex?" I ask, fighting the smirk on my lips.

She pauses her hand and shakes her head infinitesimally. "Why, yes, I do. And you refuse to help with that situation, so here I am," she says sweetly and puckers her lips. "Being friends."

"We would never work. Ever," I tell her, reaching for the pizza she's pulled out. She slides the box to me and opens up the other, smaller box, which is full of little cakes.

"Why? Because we're opposites?" she asks, lifting a cheesecake.

"That's not dinner."

"Yes, it is. Dessert before boys." She takes a large bite.

"Yes, we're opposites, but also because I'm from the wrong side of the tracks."

"We went to the same school... together," she points out.

"We did, and not once did we talk or hang out during that time."

"You never looked my way."

"No, and it was because I was fucking women, not little girls." I bite into the pizza while her eyes go wide but she reins herself in.

"Tell me some stories."

"You want to hear stories about how I fucked the rich mothers?"

"You what?" she says with shock written all over her face.

"Of course I did. I told you I wasn't good. And those mothers who I was fucking didn't approve of their kids hanging out with me."

"Oh, gosh, don't tell me they were married?"

"And worse."

"Okay, change of subject, since I know most people in this town. How was prison?" She looks at me eagerly while waiting for me to answer her.

"That's something I choose to forget. It's a part of my life I don't want to relive."

"Fuck, you're a hard egg to get information from."

I smile at her words. "And you have a potty mouth. Does your family know?"

She shrugs. "Only Rhi and Beckham."

"Do you have other friends?"

"Yes... well, no. I think Shandy is my friend. I like her."

"The one you work with?"

She nods. "Yep. And you, of course."

"You want to fuck me. There's a difference."

She leans forward. "Is there, though?" Her eyes pinch as she stares at me.

"Would it make you happy if I put you on this table, spread your legs open, and slid right in?"

She pauses mid-bite, resets herself, and then replies, "Yes." Putting down her cake, she stands. "I'm ready. Throw away," she says, opening her arms out wide. "I don't even care if that sounds desperate."

I can't help the laughter that bubbles up from inside me.

Who the fuck is this woman?

And where has she been my entire life?

"Sit down, rich girl. I'm eating." I wave her off.

Her hands fall to her hips, those dark eyes stealing my breath.

"Nope, that's unfair."

"Why don't you ask Anderson to throw you around?" I ask, recovering from her stare.

She huffs and sits. Reaching for some pizza, she bites and mumbles through a full mouth, "Don't even get me started on him."

"Now, you do have me intrigued."

"No, really... don't get me started. I wonder if I was dumb, blind, or maybe just stupid," she says while shaking her head.

"Maybe a little of each one," I offer.

She pauses and throws the crust of the pizza at me. "I'm none of them, thank you very much."

"If you say so."

"You can't tell me you've never made a mistake by being with someone before."

"That isn't up for discussion."

"Oh, come on... tell me."

"No."

"Fine, whatever. Be a dick, then."

We finish eating in silence. She checks her phone a few times, then begins to clean the mess. I watch, liking the way she moves around my house dressed in her work clothes, which are too tight for that little body.

"I can feel you watching me."

I don't deny nor confirm until she glances over her shoulder and checks me out before she comes back over.

"So, since your sex life and prison life are off the table, what can we walk about?"

"Not me."

She shakes her head. "This is us, being friends, and me learning more about you."

"You should really find another friend."

"But I've already invested so much in us." She tries to fight the smile touching her lips, but she can't beat it. "What about what you're working on? Surely you can share that?"

"It's nothing that would interest you."

"Oh my gosh, August... just fucking tell me," she snaps.

"I've made four desks for Noah's office. One for his boss, then a few of his employees, but I have more to make."

"That's great. Are they pricey?"

"Noah set the price, and they paid." I pause. "Three thousand per desk," I tell her.

"I'm sure they're worth that and more if those chairs and small table outside are anything to go by."

I didn't expect that reaction. I expected maybe I'm not worth that much. But after the first desk, they kept ordering more, and then, well, the doubt started to slowly ebb away, until delivery, that is. It's then the monster rears its ugly head until the client is happy. And so far, every client has been more than happy, which surprises me more than anything.

"They've passed my name on to more businesses. I have a contract with a few of them." I haven't told anyone but Noah, trying to keep things more internalized than I probably should. Trouble is, after being inside for so long, everything becomes a struggle, and internalizing is what you do best to keep sane.

"We need to set you up as a business." Rising from her chair, she heads outside.

Is she leaving?

Then I hear her car door shut, and she comes back, computer in hand, taking up a position on the couch. I sit next to her as she begins inputting information, asking me questions here and there. I watch her work, fascinated with the speed and complexity with which she works. Her lashes are long, which fits perfectly with her devil eyes. Her hands move fast, long delicate fingers I could have wrapped around my...

"You're staring again."

"You're beautiful to stare at."

Her head lifts at the compliment, and she turns to face me. "Thank you." She spins back to the laptop. "For that, I won't charge you, even though now I know you can afford to pay me." She's not wrong. The advance I received from the contracts is amazing. I didn't think it was possible to do something I love and make so much money out of it.

But here I am.

She continues to work away on her computer, makes a few phone calls, and all the while I watch her intently.

"Look how far you've come," she says, shutting the computer after having set me up in business, it seems. "You should be proud of yourself, August Trouble. Because I am."

I have no response to those words.

Not once has anyone ever said they were proud of me. That's something someone like me never hears uttered.

"August." She touches my arm.

Maybe it's her words, maybe it is just her.

But what I do next, I told myself I would never do again.

But for some reason, I can't help myself.

I'm a starving man, and she has served up my three-course meal.

CHAPTER
19

Rylee

I should be pushing him away. I know this. But when August's lips touch mine, and he pushes me backward on the couch, I'm a helpless woman. Besides, it wasn't my idea to keep things platonic between us. That was all him.

So when his hand slides up my skirt I know, I just know, we're more than friends.

Maybe friends with benefits?

August's lips capture mine.

And in that moment, nothing is more

important than keeping that kiss going, even when his fingers slide past my panties and straight to where I want them. I pause only for a second, my lips frozen in pleasure before I bite down on his bottom lip. His fingers start pumping inside of me while he makes these amazing noises with his mouth.

Just as I go to reach between us to touch him, something bangs on the door, loudly. It's as if it's being kicked. August stops abruptly, then is off me in the next second before he moves to the door with a bat in his hand, freezing mid-step as the door is kicked in. Two men stand there, facing me, both wearing black balaclavas. I can't see their eyes, but I feel them all over my skin as I remain immobile on the couch, for some reason just blinking.

"Look what we got," one of them says, as the other attempts to move forward in my direction. August swings the bat, knocking the one closest to him in the backs of his knees, forcing him to the floor with a loud scream.

I shiver, covering my ears at the crack the bat made when it connected with his bones.

"What the…" Before the other can do anything, I open my eyes to see August do the same thing with him, but the crack isn't as loud as the guy jumps, getting whacked in only one leg instead of both.

"August." I say his name, but he doesn't hear

me as he rushes over to the closest one, tears the mask off, and bends down, his hand gripping the intruder's shirt, and he pulls him up, making him whine out in pain.

"You are either brave or stupid to try to enter my house. Which is it?" August growls.

I stand on shaky legs and stare at August. I've never seen this side of him.

He's so... dark.

His fists move fast as he punches the dude's face. I hear the crack of bone and flinch at the sound.

"August." I say his name again, but he doesn't seem to hear me.

"You stepped into the wrong house, fucker." He hits again, knocking the guy unconscious. The one whose leg he hit pulls something from his pocket. I freeze, and a scream rips out of my mouth when I realize it's a gun.

August pauses but only for a split second, which is enough time for the guy to shoot, but because he's on the floor and August is fast, it only hits August's shoulder. August barely registers the bullet, not even recoiling when it strikes him. He keeps moving and knocks the gun from the guy's hand. Then, in one fast movement that I've only seen in the movies, he knocks that guy unconscious as well.

August stands, touches his shoulder, then looks over at me. "You should leave."

I shake my head, knowing I'm not going to leave him.

"Leave, Rylee." I can't even get caught on the fact that he's used my name because the blood that's flowing out of his wound has me moving toward him not away from him. Reaching out, I want to touch him to make sure he's okay. I step over the bodies that lie on the floor and gently touch his shoulder.

His voice becomes softer when my hand caresses him. "Leave," he almost whispers.

"No," I tell him. I know it won't be long before the police arrive. After all, a gunshot would have been heard by the neighbors.

Not knowing how long we've been standing there, time seems to be going in slow motion right now. My heart is hammering in my chest, and my mind seems to be struggling between wanting to run and wanting to stay. The battle is constant, but somehow, I manage to keep grounded. Somehow keeping myself as centered as I can.

Sirens, I hear them, and they are coming this way.

Shock.

Alarm.

Panicked.

All feelings, all genuine, but all dismissed as quickly as they arrive when two police officers appear through the broken door. The two unconscious men are immediately spotted, so they both pull their weapons from their holsters.

"On the floor, both of you. Very slowly." I quickly glance at August, who simply nods, doing what they say. One of them speaks into the radio on his shoulder before another police car arrives. When I check outside through the floor-to-ceiling window, I see the neighbors coming out on their front yards, and they're all looking this way.

"August." Paige's father is standing there, hand on his gun but not raised like the other two. "What's going on here?"

"He's hurt. They shot August," I tell Glenn.

His eyes fall to August, who appears to be having trouble keeping his eyes open.

"An ambulance is on its way. Can you tell me what happened?" Glenn asks.

My eyes fall to the men lying beside me.

One of them starts to move, and I jump up, not wanting to be anywhere near them.

"They broke into the house through the door. See, it's broken. August..." I look and find his eyes are opening and closing, but he's trying to keep an eye on the man whose eyes are still shut. "They didn't get far, but one had a gun." I point at the gun one of the officers is standing in front of. "He shot August. August did nothing wrong. We were having dinner when they—"

"Thank you, Rylee. I'll need you to come to the station to make a statement, but other than that, you're free to go." I step back and look at August, who's still on the floor and bleeding badly.

"What about August?" I ask.

"He'll have to come with us after he goes to the hospital."

"But, he did nothing wrong," I tell Glenn.

He doesn't answer.

So I reach for my phone and call my sister, who picks up straight away.

"Is Noah with you?"

"Umm... yes," she says, her voice confused.

"Can you put him on, please?"

She doesn't ask any questions, which I'm thankful for.

"Rylee, everything okay?" Noah's voice echoes through the phone.

"No. Two people just tried to break into August's house, and he got shot. The police are taking him in for some reason after he's been to the hospital. Can you help?"

"Where are you?"

"Still at his house."

"Don't move. Collect your things. I'll be there soon."

As I hang up, the ambulance arrives, and an officer puts cuffs on August, making him groan as they jostle around his wounded shoulder. He doesn't say a word, just goes with it as they carry him off to the ambulance.

"I want to go with him," I say to a different officer, who adamantly shakes his head.

"No can do, miss." He blocks my path as the ambulance drives away. I watch as the ambulance turns the corner then Noah's car pulls up. My sister rushes through the house to get to me. Her way is clear now that the other two men have been moved, cuffed, and taken away in another ambulance.

"Ry… oh my God, what's happening?" She checks the blood on the floor then wraps her arms around me.

"Got your things?" Noah asks while scanning the house.

I nod, and Rhianna pulls me out and to the car.

Noah gets in and drives while I tell them everything that happened. Noah nods but doesn't say a single word as he comes to a stop out the front of our apartment.

"I want to go with you."

"No. I'll bring him back here, though. You need to go inside and wash up." I glance down at myself and see my white blouse has blood splatters all over it.

"I can change real quick."

"It will be easier if you aren't there. Let me handle it."

Rhianna gets out of the car, then comes around and opens my door. "Come on, Noah will handle it."

I nod even though I don't want to and get out, looking back down at Noah. "Make sure he's okay."

Noah nods as I shut the car door, then he drives away.

"Ry, are you okay?" Concern laces her voice, and a shiver racks my body.

"I think so. Holy shit, Rhi. Holy shit," I say while shaking my head.

She pulls me to her for a hug, not caring at all that I have blood all over me while I cry on her shoulder.

"It'll be okay. You're okay."

I nod on her shoulder, then pull back. "I need to shower. Then we need to call Noah to see what's happening."

She doesn't argue with me.

She knows me.

Better than anyone on his planet.

When I get to the shower and strip the clothes from my body, Rhianna picks up the shirt and carries it out before she comes back in and sits on the toilet while I shower.

"Ry, do you like him?"

I pause while washing my face, not even caring that some of the wetness now on my face is my own tears.

"Yes," I answer quite simply because I know what she's asking. Not if I like him as a friend, but do I want more.

"Does he like you?"

"I'm not sure how to answer that."

She pulls back the shower door. "It's a yes or no. Does *he* like *you?*"

"I think so." I shrug. "I mean... as far as I am aware, apart from Paige, I'm his only friend."

"But it's not friends you want to be, right? You want more?"

"Yes, I want more." I don't bother lying because she'll know I am. Rhianna nods and sits again, leaving the shower door open. It doesn't bother me. Our bodies are exactly the same, there isn't much difference between us apart from our personalities.

Her phone starts ringing, and I hold my breath as she answers and puts it on speaker.

"Hey."

"They fixed him up, but he's refusing to stay

the night, and the officers said he can't go back to his place."

"Bring him here." I hear myself saying before I even have time to think.

"Rhianna?" Noah asks her.

I look at her.

"Yes, bring him back here," she confirms.

"Okay, we'll be there soon." He hangs up, and Rhianna focuses back on me.

"Are you sure you know what you're doing?"

"No, but he has nowhere else to go," I say, closing the door and stepping back under the shower spray. I let the warm water wash away every emotion, and then I let it swirl down the drain. They say water has a calming effect, and in some countries, it's even used to cleanse your soul.

Shaking out of my stupor, I shut off the faucet and step out.

Rhianna is still there waiting, but she's holding out a towel for me.

"Do you want coffee?" I shake my head as she stands. "Anything?" Again, I shake my head. My words seem to be lost right now. "Okay, get dressed. They won't be long." She spins around and strolls out, and I head to my room, shutting the door behind me. I lie on the bed, face-first, still wrapped in my towel.

What just happened?

What just happened?

I've never even seen a gun before. Yet, I just saw someone get shot.

I've never even been in a fight. Yet, I just saw someone beat someone else until they lost consciousness.

It should make me afraid of August.

I should be scared.

But I know what the devil really looks like, and usually, he's dressed to impress and ready to kill. It's those types of men who hurt women.

Not him.

Not August.

Not once have I felt unsafe around him or that he could cause me harm in any way. Not even when he was dealing with the intruders.

I felt safe.

I feel safe.

He protects me, and I know no one would be able to harm me if he was there.

Closing my eyes, I squeeze them tight, hoping to rid myself of the images of August's actions.

There's hurt.

Pain.

I'm immobile.

And soon, I just pass out.

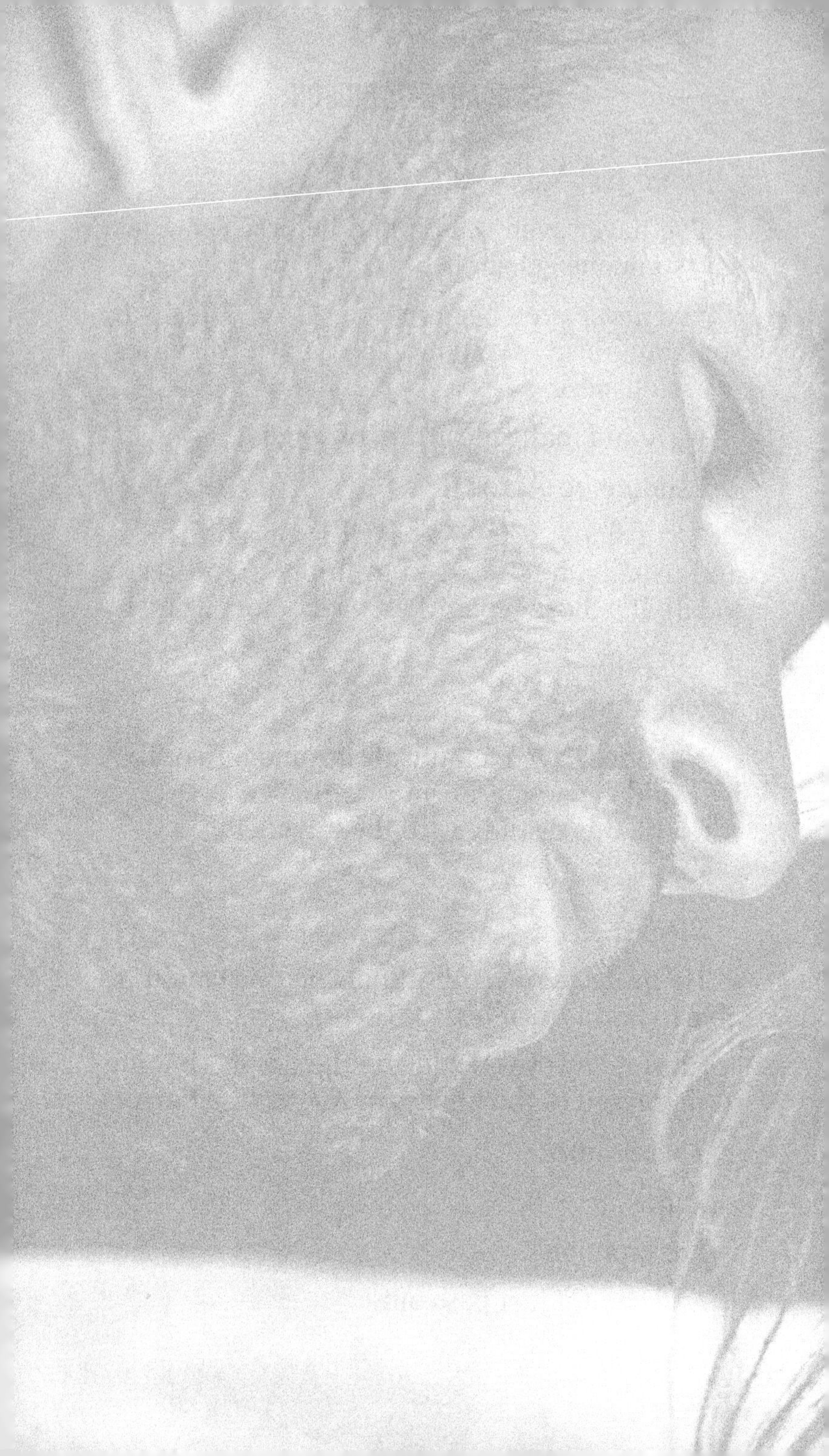

CHAPTER 20

August

"Hey, August," Rhianna says, opening the door.

Noah nods for me to head inside first, and I pass Rhianna as I step in. My eyes scan the apartment and don't see Rylee.

"She's in her room if you want to go in."

I know which room is hers, so I head there, tapping on the door. When she doesn't answer, I open it a fraction and see her wrapped in nothing but a towel, asleep on the bed, curled in a ball.

I hear Noah talking to Rhianna, explaining that I have to go back tomorrow with Rylee for another round of questioning.

All I can do is stand there and watch Rylee sleeping. I don't dare enter the room, unwilling to wake her.

"You can go in," Rhianna says softly to me.

I move to step back and close the door when Rylee's eyes open. Those eyes trap me, snare me with their intensity, and without even thinking, I step into the room and shut the door behind me.

"Are you sore?" she asks, sitting up on the bed, the towel almost falling off. She taps the empty spot on the bed next to her. "I'm really tired, August. Really tired," she says, and I can hear the pain in her voice.

Did I cause that pain?

I glance at the clock. It's almost three in the morning. The adrenaline that would've been running through her system must be gone by now. I kick my shoes off and climb into bed, so my injured side is to the edge, then I pull her up so her head lies on my shoulder.

"Go to sleep."

She curls herself around me, and within seconds she's fast asleep, smelling like strawberries and all things Rylee.

I lie there listening to her soft snores, wondering what the fuck I'm going to do about this situation.

Josh won't stop.

I know he won't.

He was the one who sent those thugs. I recognized them as his men as soon as they entered the house.

I attempt to pull my arm out from under her, but she pushes herself closer into my side. So, I stay that way, falling in and out of asleep until I finally close my eyes and pass out listening to her breathing.

She's awake before me. When I finally open my eyes, I find her sitting on the end of the bed. The towel she had on still covers her body as she sits there quietly with her head down.

"Rich girl." She spins around to face me, her eyes red and her face bare of any makeup.

She's simply beautiful.

"Are you in pain?" she asks, her eyes going straight to my shoulder.

"No," I answer, sitting up.

She stands, heads to her closet, and reaches for a dress, dropping the towel and changing in front of me. "We have to go to the police station."

"You don't have to."

She turns, now dressed, and shakes her head. "I do. Now come... Noah's waiting for us."

I catch her wrist as she walks past me on her way to the door, and a tear leaves her eye when she turns back to me. "I told you to stay away from me. I'm nothing but trouble."

"You aren't. Stop saying that. Stop doing that. There's nothing wrong with you. It's those who you used to associate with." She pulls her arm free, opens the door, and steps out.

I take a minute, putting my shoes on before I join her. When I do, Noah and Rylee's sister are standing at the kitchen counter talking while Rylee makes a coffee. After she's done, she hands it to me then goes back to make a cup for herself.

"How are you feeling today?" Noah asks, nodding to my shoulder.

"I'll be fine."

"Good to hear. Because the station has already called asking when you're going to be there."

My phone starts ringing. I didn't even realize I had it with me.

"Noah grabbed it," Rhianna says at my look of confusion.

Picking it up, I answer the call. "August, oh, good. I've been calling, but you haven't been picking up," Paige says. "Are you at Rhianna's?"

"Yes."

"I'm at the door."

I hear a knock, and Rylee opens the door to her brother and Paige standing there. Paige runs inside and wraps her arms around my waist, hugging me tight.

"Where does your father think you are?"

"With Beckham," she says, pulling back. "Technically, I am. I am not lying."

"You shouldn't be here." I look over to Beckham who's talking to Rylee. "Take her home."

Beckham glances at Paige. "I told her she wasn't allowed to come. Her father even said so," he states, making my eyes go to Paige.

"This is what got you into trouble last time." She glances down at my words, avoiding eye contact. "Take her home, Beckham," I tell him. "I'll call you later, Paige."

She nods and says no more, then marches out with Beckham.

"That was a little harsh," Rhianna says.

I ignore her and ask Noah, "Should we go now?"

"Yeah, if you're ready."

My answer is a nod.

Once we get to the parking lot, I watch Paige get into her boyfriend's car and drive away.

"You can ride with me," Rylee says, coming up behind me.

"No."

"You *will* ride with me, August Trouble. Get in my fucking car. *Now*. So we can talk." I hear a faint giggle and know it's her sister, so I sigh and get in. When we're both buckled in, she starts the car and takes off with a squeal of her wheels.

"What do you want to talk about?" I ask, checking her out in my peripheral vision, while both of her hands are on the steering wheel and she's clenching it tightly.

"I want to know what the fuck is going on. Tell me... who those men were, and why they were at your house."

I scrub my hand down my face.

Fuck! I'm still so tired, even if it was one of the best night's sleep I've had in a long time, lying next to her. I wonder if it was her bed or her.

"What?"

"Why did those men come into your house?

Were they going to kill you?" she asks, her knuckles now white as she grasps the steering wheel.

"No. They came to hurt me. Scare me into doing what Josh wants me to do."

Her eyes flick to me. "Josh, the guy from the bar? What's he got to do with anything?"

"Yes, him. He runs the drugs in this city. No one can sell without going through him for product. There are other things he does, too."

"Did you deal?"

"Yes, amongst other things."

She nods at my answer. "Thank you for that. Now... tell me... what does he want you to do?"

"He wants me to work for him..." I pause as we pull up to the police station. "He also wanted to teach me a lesson for the last time I told him no." She takes a heavy breath. "I ended up in prison," I say while getting out and shutting the door and rushing off.

Before I reach the steps, she runs up beside me then blocks my way. "He set you up?"

"Of course he did."

"You never robbed that store? Stole all that money? Hurt that man?"

"No. I was there, but no, I didn't do any of that shit."

"I believe you." She says the words with such conviction and without a shred of evidence. Not once have I had someone believe in me so blindly—simply by my word. I'm not sure what to do with that.

"Thanks," I manage to say. I push past her then head up the stairs to the police station.

I didn't find out about the man who was robbed being seriously hurt until it was too late. But the biggest crime was destroying the property of someone wealthy and connected, plus stealing. Even though my fingerprints were on nothing, it didn't seem to matter.

Josh had set me up.

I had to pay the price.

It was *his* punishment for me wanting to get out of this town and to stop working for him. The asshole didn't like that I wanted out. I always managed to get the best outcomes for Josh from all his workers. His dealers never turned me down when it came to paying. And he's now lost his edge since I've been gone. Not many people are scared of him now. He's getting older, and the police are getting wiser.

"August." I turn and look down at her. She's standing at the bottom of the steps, staring up at me. "I like you," she whispers, but I can hear every word she says. "No more friends."

Before I can reply, Glenn steps in front of me.

"Good to see you're here." He nods and holds open the door for me.

And with that, I look away from her, and it pains me to do so.

Noah pulls up to my place and parks the car in the driveway.

"She cares for you, you know."

"I know," I say, getting out.

I'm tired.

I'm over today.

Questions, questions, and more fucking questions. I fucking hate it. Last time, before they threw me away, there was no chance of them believing me. So my hope is slim that somehow I won't become the bad guy in this situation too, even though *they* broke into *my* house.

"Get off the floor."

She spins on her hands and knees then squeals.

Fuck, probably shouldn't have snuck up on her like that.

"August, you scared me."

"Yeah, well, you shouldn't be on the fucking

floor." She gets up and wipes her hands on her skirt.

"I wanted to clean the mess. Noah said you'd be gone all day. I figured you didn't want to deal with this bullshit as well."

I've never had someone care so much for me, so much so that I take a step back from her. She sees what I do and steps closer. Not caring that I'm trying to put distance between us at all.

"You've never had anyone help you, or even been in a relationship, have you?"

"No, and I don't want one."

"They can be good."

"And you're speaking from experience?" I bite back at her.

She takes that hit hard and steps back. "I may be the stupid one who stayed in a relationship that was well past its end date, but at least I tried. I tried to give myself to someone, to love them, because as humans we all need love, August."

"Not everyone."

Rylee's eyes are hard as she steps up to me, until her feet are touching my shoes, and reaches for my face, pulling it so we're at eye level.

I let her.

"Yes, even you. You need it more than anyone

I've ever met." She lets go and reaches for her shoes, slips them on, and steps off past me. "Goodnight, August. If you need me, you know where I live."

I watch her walk out and drive away.

After she's gone, I check around and note that she has cleaned the house. You can't even tell that blood coated my entryway any longer.

Goddammit.!

I slam the door shut and punch the wall. Hard as fuck.

CHAPTER 21

"Move over," a deep voice rumbles next to me.

I open my eyes, but my room is dark. I know who it is straight away, though. His smell envelops me, and his hands wrap around my mid-section, putting me at ease with his touch.

"August," I say, but he doesn't say anything back, just pulls me to him. I go because I can't think of a better place to be than wrapped in his arms. My head lies on his chest as his hand plays circles on my back. "Are you sore?" I ask him, my eyes lifting to his other shoulder where I know he was hurt.

"Only a little," he finally says.

I sit up and flick the lamp on next to the bed so I can see him. August isn't wearing his shirt and only has on a pair of boxers. I reach my hand down and touch his taut stomach, and his eyes close for a brief second before they open again, staring at me.

"What are you doing to me?"

I don't think he realizes he's voiced those words out loud. I stand and drop my nightgown to the floor, and his eyes trace every part of me, watching me eagerly but not once moving. His eyes are drunk on me.

"When your hands touch me, it makes me feel alive," I tell him.

Stepping to his side of the bed, I reach for his hand and place it on my stomach.

"Even the simplest touch." I drop my hand, but his hand stays where it is. I watch him draw circles on my skin before his hand drops between my legs, tracing me.

"You don't want this," he says, but his hands don't leave my body. "It would be a grave mistake to want more from me." His finger enters me and slides back out. "You're the rich girl from the right side of the tracks. I *will* be your worst mistake."

"Or my favorite one yet," I reply as his fingers grip my waist. I climb on his lap, and he grips me tighter. "Tell me, August, do you feel anything when I touch you?"

He stays silent as I watch him. I wait, not daring to breathe.

I'm eager for his words.

Hungry for them.

He never minces his words with me. It's one of the things I like about him.

"You don't want my words, rich girl. You want my body."

"I want both. Now, tell me the truth... stop hiding behind them."

He sits up fast, his chest coming into contact with mine as his hands wrap around my back, making it difficult for even a slither of air to come between us. He leans forward so our lips are almost within reach. "When you touch me, rich girl, all my pain is gone. It's like it never existed. And you make me feel whole again." I gasp at his words. "Is that what you want? You want me to become that person? One who tells you all those things?"

"No, I like you the way you are. But sometimes..." I lean forward, placing a soft kiss on his lips, "... it's nice to know I'm not on this rollercoaster alone." I kiss him with full force, passionate and strong, and he lets me. Not once does he pull back, and I try to be careful that I don't hurt his shoulder when I touch him.

August moans into my mouth, and I push up on him until he reaches between us and positions himself right where I need him.

"Dangerous game," he whispers as I lower myself onto him.

"All the best games are," I murmur back.

August isn't next to me when I wake. My bed is empty, and standing at my door is Rhianna. She holds two cups of coffee in her hands.

"You two were noisy last night. At least now I know we have that in common as well." She laughs, stepping in and handing me a mug. I sit, taking the drink from her. "He had to leave with Noah to finalize some things. And you, missy, have to go to work. Dad called for you."

"Shit." I check the time and see it's way past the time I'm meant to start. I'm late. I'm never late. "Was he mad?" I ask, running around and reaching for the closest clothes I can find.

"No. He was worried."

I'm over two hours late, that's not like me. Ever. I slept hard. I haven't slept in for so long, and it felt so good.

The door opens, and Rhi turns and moves out of the way and heads into the bathroom as August strolls in. I smile as I pull on my blouse and throw around a few things in my closet trying to find an appropriate pair of shoes. "I have to get to work. I'm late," I tell him.

August folds his arms over his chest, leans back against the door, and watches me run around getting dressed. I manage to throw my hair up in a presentable bun as I slide my heels on.

"Do you have plans today? Maybe we can do lunch?" I ask August, making him scrunch his nose up.

There's a knock on the front door. We both turn to look, but I can't see the door from my room, though August can. He instantly straightens, his arms falling to his sides. I step past him to see Anderson standing there, his eyes landing on August then falling to me.

"Rylee." Noah turns to me, having answered the door, as my sister steps out of the bathroom.

"Oh, hell no. You should know better than to come to my house, you fuckhead," she screams.

"Rylee, it's Catrina," he says.

"What's wrong?"

"She had a heart attack. Can you come?"

August's hand reaches out and captures mine.

Anderson's eyes drop to the movement.

Catrina is Anderson's grandmother, and she's a good woman. Unlike his own mother. Anderson's eyes are red, which they should be.

"Is she okay?" I ask because I do care. I like her—a lot. I have always had time for her.

"No. They don't think she'll make it another hour."

"Then, why are you here?" Rhianna snaps.

I pull my arm free of August's hold and reach for my keys.

"She asked for Rylee," he says simply.

"Don't..." August says next to me.

I turn to August and see him watching Anderson.

"I'm coming." I don't look back as I walk out the door because I don't want to see the look of disappointment on any of their faces.

When we get to our cars, Anderson holds open the passenger door of his car.

"I should take my own car."

"Please, just get in. I'm tired, Rylee."

I nod, not wanting to argue with him. If his grandmother is dying, the last thing he would want to do is argue with me. So, I slide in, and he starts driving.

"How's your mother?"

"Why was August Trouble at your house?" he replies, his hands squeezing the steering wheel.

"What? You don't get to ask that! Anderson, how's your mother?" I ask again.

"Do you take me for a fool?" he spits, and it's then I note he's not driving the right way to the hospital.

"Anderson," I say, reaching for my phone in my bag. He snatches it from my hand and throws it in the back seat.

"You can't call him to come to your rescue. He is scum. The things he used to do. How could you associate yourself with someone like that?" he says almost calmly. "You were meant to be my wife…" now his voice is rising to almost a scream, "…and now you make *me* look like trash." He keeps on driving. Speeding down the street. My anxiety level rising with each second that passes.

"Where are we going?" My hands are shaking, and my eyes seem to be skirting around, trying to work out a way out of this situation I now find myself in. If I open the door, I could jump, but the car's going fast and the outcome might not be good.

"To make you remember you love *me*, and *we* are *it* for each other."

"Anderson, pull over. Let me out of this car *right now*."

"No can do, Rylee. You're *mine,* and you're delusional if you think you belong to someone else. I let you have your fun with the trash, now it can take itself out, and you can come back home with me, where you were meant to be all along."

He turns down a dirt path.

I know instantly where he's taking me, to the place where I lost my virginity to him. It was a terrible night. I wasn't ready. And now when I look back, I can see he pressured me into it.

How very different the two men are.

Here I was, throwing myself at August and he respectfully waited.

Where Anderson pressures me into things, like right now. He's lying to get what he wants.

His hand touches my thigh and I jump, pushing his hand away, almost swatting it like a fly.

"Where is your girlfriend? You should be with her, Anderson."

"She isn't my girlfriend. *You are,*" he says the last two words through gritted teeth.

His hair's a mess. I assumed it was because he was upset, but now I realize it was all a ploy. I see his phone is sitting between us.

"I am not your girlfriend. We don't work, Anderson. You cheated every chance you got. I was unhappy and going through the motions with you. Don't you think we deserve more? You could be happy with someone else."

"No. You're what makes me happy."

"Happy people don't cheat, Anderson," I tell him as he slows the car down.

"Is that what it will take? For me *not* to cheat?" he asks, glancing my way. "I'll do it, but that means you will have to fuck me more, Rylee. Stop pushing me away."

"That's not what I meant, and you know it. I *don't* want you."

"You want him," he growls. "Prison's trash."

The car comes to a stop, and he unlocks the door, getting out. As soon as he does, I reach for my bag, knocking his phone into it. I open my door and start sprinting. It's muddy because it rained last night, and because I'm in heels my feet keep slipping.

I hear him laugh behind me.

"I like to play catch and fuck. Is this what this is, Rylee? A new game? This is why I love you. You are always coming up with new things."

I gasp as I try to catch my breath and keep going. I reach for his phone in my bag and try to remember August's number without Anderson seeing what I'm doing. He answers, and just as he does, I'm tackled from behind and fall head-first into the mud. It covers my face and knocks the wind out of me as well. His laugh is the first thing I hear when I can't hear anything other than my own breathing and a ringing in my ears.

"How do you want it?" he asks, tearing at my shirt.

"Get the hell off me," I scream.

He leans down and comes close to my ear. "I'll get off on you, then in you, then maybe I'll christen your ass as well."

I scream but it's useless.

We're out in the middle of nowhere, and unless it's nighttime and the teenagers want to get lucky, no one comes out here during the day.

"Fuck you," I say. Reaching between us, I hit him as hard as I can on his cock. He yelps and falls to the side. I keep the phone in hand and run again. This time I don't hear his footsteps behind me, but that doesn't slow my pace at all, even though I'm wearing one heel and stockings. My skirt is bunched up, and the farther I run, the more adrenaline hits me. I hear a faint noise and raise the phone to my ear.

"Rylee, fuck! Tell me you're alive." I hear August's voice.

I slow down, spin, and check around to see no sign of Anderson.

"Rylee," he screams into the phone.

"Rylee, tell me where you are." My sister's calm voice breaks through my daze.

"The hill," I manage to get out.

"I know where that is. Call the police," Rhianna says.

I don't stop moving.

I can't stop moving.

I know if he looks hard enough, Anderson will find me again, and when he does he'll be so damn angry.

"Rylee!" The asshole screams my name, and it echoes through the woods. "I'm coming for what's mine." Oh my God, he sounds crazed, like some sort of lunatic that has escaped from an asylum and is coming for me like in the movies.

I wipe at my face and don't stop.

I won't stop.

I can't stop.

CHAPTER 22

"I know where she is," Rhianna says, grabbing her keys and running out the door. I'm right behind her, with Noah on my heels. As soon as we're in the car and moving, Noah starts making calls. The first call is straight to Glenn, telling him where we're going. When he finally hangs up, he turns back to me.

"If you see Anderson, you stay away. Do. You. Understand?"

I don't answer.

How can I answer that?

If he's hurt her, I'll kill him. And I'll have no remorse for doing so.

How can you hurt someone as nice as Rylee?

"August... Do. You. Hear. Me? If you touch him, you will go straight back to prison."

Still, I don't answer.

I see the hill, and when we arrive, a police car drives up behind us.

Glenn gets out as we rush over to Anderson's vehicle.

"He went in there. Look..." Rhianna points to the footprints that lead into the forest. I start running, following them. I hear their footsteps behind me, but I don't stop. Nothing could stop me.

"Rylee..." I hear him say her name.

He's taunting her.

Tormenting her.

My feet don't slow as I come up behind him. When he turns around, shock is written on his face as I bend over and slam him into the ground with as much force as I can. Hands grab at me as I get up.

"Leave him! Go and find Rylee," Glenn says, looking down at Anderson on the ground. Glenn hovers over him scanning around.

Rhianna starts yelling her name.

"Where is she?" she says in desperation.

We all split up, and as I go farther in, I find one of her heels on the ground.

"Rylee." I don't yell it. There isn't anyone else in these woods but us. And it's dead quiet. It's as if the birds know they need to be silent right now.

"August."

I turn to find her hunched under a tree, her blouse is torn, and her face is covered in mud. I reach for her, pulling her up. She stands on shaky legs and drops her head to my chest.

"Anderson..."

Brushing my hands down her hair, I try to soothe her, but it's hard when you have never had to do something like this before. My mother never cuddled me, and the only people in my life that have are Paige and Rylee. But I squeeze her to me so she knows she's safe.

"I'm going to pick you up now," I tell her, pulling back.

"You can't, your shoulder," she says, touching it ever so lightly.

"I'm fine," I tell her as I lift.

She lets me and I make our way back out.

Rhianna is the first to spot us. "Rylee," she screams and runs over.

Glenn's head turns, and I see he has Anderson in cuffs waiting at the car.

Noah stands with them, showing something on his phone.

"Noah recorded it. He recorded it all," Rhianna says as I breathe a sigh of relief. They didn't hear it all, but I'm guessing they've heard enough. And I'm sure he said way worse while we weren't on the phone.

"Rylee, do I need to call an ambulance?" Glenn asks.

"No. No, please don't," she begs.

I scan her body for injuries, noticing her scraped knees. "You should at least see a doctor."

"I don't want to. I want to go to work. I want to go and change, shower, and go to work."

Rhianna looks confused.

"Work?" she says to her sister. "Ry, you need time. Dad will understand."

"August, you can put me down." I do as she says but keep my hand on her lower back.

"I need to get to work. I need this to not have ever happened."

"But it did, and Anderson is going into the station because of it." Her eyes fall to Anderson, who's in the car now, his beady eyes watching us, smirking.

"You can work at my house," I offer.

"No, I have paperwork I need to get."

"We can get it, and you can work from my house," I tell her again.

She doesn't argue this time. She simply nods.

She steps out of the bathroom dressed in my shirt. It reaches her thighs and looks good on her.

"Feel better?"

She nods, brushing a dark lock behind her ear. "My knees sting a bit."

When I check, they are grazed badly. "I have some stuff for that."

"I can't go into work dressed like this," she says, gesturing to what she's wearing.

The doorbell rings, and I stroll over to answer it and see her friend, Shandy, on the other side. "Thanks for coming," I tell her, letting her step in.

Her eyes fall to Rylee, then to me. "Is she okay?" she whispers, and I give her a nod.

"I can hear you," Rylee says, walking over.

Shandy offers her a shy smile and hands her computer over. "I told your father that you needed it for a meeting."

"Thank you."

They stand there awkwardly for a few seconds before I step away into the kitchen but I can still hear what they're saying.

"Did you need me to get you anything else?"

"No, I should be fine."

"I have you covered at work for today and tomorrow. Would it be okay if I came over after work with maybe some wine... you know, if you feel up to it?"

"This isn't my place."

"Oh," she says, surprised. "I didn't know. Sorry."

"You're welcome to come over," I say as I pass by on my way out to the shed.

Rylee offers me a small smile as I head out the back door. I hear them talking but try to focus on the desk that I'm making. I only have two left for my current contract, and so far, I'm well in advance of the agreed delivery date, which I hope will be good for getting some more recommendations.

"You didn't have to do that," Rylee says, surprising me a short time later.

I drop my sander and turn to her. She has a glass of water in her hand.

"What did he do to you?"

She shakes her head. "Nothing I can't handle."

"You don't have to handle it," I growl.

"You sound like you care, August. You better watch yourself before you catch real feelings."

"Who said they haven't already been caught?"

Her smile could light up the darkest skies, even with the pain radiating through her tormented eyes. How someone so perfect can have such haunted eyes, I really don't understand.

"I think I fell a little all those years ago. Back then, you were an asshole, and now, even more so." She steps in and sits on one of the seats in my shed. "Thank you for inviting Shandy around later. You didn't have to do that. This isn't my house, and I'm fine if you want to take me back to my place."

"You've had a big week."

"As have you," she replies.

"That was the scariest thing to ever happen to me, and I have had a lot of shit to deal with in my life. To hear you scream into that phone... I wanted to kill him. If Glenn weren't there, I probably would have," I tell her honestly.

"I'm glad you didn't. I like having you out here in the real world."

"Even with all the crazy?" I ask.

"It's a hundred times better than what I had to deal with before, so yes. Even with all the crazy." I step up to her, hands in gloves, and lean forward, letting my lips touch hers. She kisses me back, and when I pull away she's smiling.

I like her smiles.

"Shandy thinks you're cute," she says when I pick up my sander to continue work.

"And what do you think?" I ask, teasing.

She opens her computer. "I mean... the view would be better for me, you know, more relaxing... if you lost the shirt." She winks and raises an eyebrow.

I tear off my shirt, toss it at her, and wink back before going back to work.

She stays with me in the shed all afternoon, only leaving to grab some bottled water, then coming straight back.

We work in silence.

Together.

Occasionally she throws me a few questions, but other than that, we do our own thing.

I like having her around.

Actually, I like it a lot.

Even if it can never work between us.

I see her move as she closes her computer. She stands, walks over to where I'm working, and runs her hand over the desk.

"What you create... it's beautiful. The design, the shape... it's so unique." I hear what she's saying, but my eyes are firmly on her. "It's not shaped like a normal desk. It has grooves and isn't a rectangle. What made you..." she trails off when she looks up at me, sucking in a breath. "What?"

My gaze slides over hers. "You are astonishingly beautiful, do you know that?"

She flicks her hair over her shoulder, a shy smile playing on her lips. "You aren't too bad yourself, August." She winks.

CHAPTER 23

Rylee

I stayed the night, and he was respectful the whole time. When I woke the next morning, he wasn't there, but at the end of the bed was a bag full of clothes and my phone, fully charged.

I get dressed because today, I really need to get to the office. Despite what others think, I like my job. I'm good at it, and to be perfectly clear, I can't let fear dictate my life.

Stepping down his stairs, I find August in the kitchen with Noah.

Noah offers me a kind smile before he turns back to August, whose eyes are eating me up.

His words from last night slam into me.

"Noah said Anderson spent the night in jail. His parents managed to get him out today, but if you press charges, due to the overwhelming evidence, it could go further," August says.

"Press charges? He's having a baby."

"Do you think he's harmless?" Noah asks.

I bite my lip and look down. "No."

"Do you think he would do this again… hurt another woman?"

"Yes," I say with a heavy breath.

"And you can live with that? What if the next woman he did it to, he killed?" Noah's in full lawyer mode when he says, "I've seen it in the courts time and time again, Rylee. As a friend, and someone who cares about you, I want you to press charges, but I won't pressure you if you don't want to."

"His family will hate me."

"They already do. They asked this morning what charges they can lay on you."

"Me?" My voice squeaks in surprise.

Noah nods. "They have nothing, so don't worry. But they would do it to you if they could, if they could find anything."

I watch August as he stares down at his coffee while he listens.

"Do you think I should?" I ask August.

"Yes," he says without missing one single beat. "But it's your choice. Do or don't. I won't judge you either way."

"I have to get to work," I say, not answering either of them right now because I need to think.

"Your car is here," Noah says, handing me my keys.

"Thank you." August nods. He knows I mean thank you for a lot more than what he did for me, but for also looking after me and even for inviting Shandy over. He cooked for us last night, and it felt comfortable. Not once did I feel as if he had eyes for Shandy, not like it did with Anderson. It was nice, and I've never had a lot of nice with a man before him.

When I leave, I drive straight to work.

Before I'm even settled in my office, my father rushes in, shutting the door behind him.

"Why are you here?" he barks. "Are you okay?" He's in front of me in three strides, looking me over. "I'm going to throw everything I have at that family, and that kid will never see the light of day again." He shakes his head and walks out without even waiting for a reply. I raise an eyebrow and push back in my chair.

"Hey." Shandy pops her head in a little later. "You look better, refreshed," she says, as she takes a seat on the opposite side of my desk. "You've had a few calls this morning. Warning... one was your mother."

I shiver at those words. Shandy knows not to accept calls from my mother unless it's at the end of the business day. Mom talks too much and doesn't understand that my life isn't spent wondering which color my bedspread should be.

"Did she say what she wanted?"

"She wanted to know if you'd be in the office today."

"Okay."

That's odd.

But okay.

My mother has always wanted me to work until I'm married and have kids, then she wants me to be like her and stay at home. Yeah, that was never going to happen. I like to work. I like making my own money.

"Hey, I know it's not my place, but are you all right?"

"I'm okay. Thanks for asking."

And I am.

Each day is better than the last. And having August near makes it a little bit sweeter. I'm not sure how he can do that, make my life better, but he does.

And I like it.

I like him.

"You aren't pressing charges?" I glance up to see my mother standing in the doorway of my office with Shandy behind her, mouthing she's sorry.

"Come in. Take a seat, why don't you?" I wave at the seat in front of me and she steps farther in.

"You aren't pressing charges, Rylee," she says again, and it's not a question, which I thought it was the first time she said it. Now, I know it's a direction. My mother places her bag on my desk, her hands on her hips.

Shandy shuts the door quietly behind her, and I take a deep breath, preparing for the onslaught of what my mother is going to send my way.

"And why would that be?"

"Because his family is powerful. Any disagreement with them could be detrimental to us." She stares at me, and somehow I see a mixture of determination and hope flash in her eyes. *Is she fucking serious?*

"Do you know what he did?" I ask her incredulously.

She smooths her hand over her skirt before she sits in front of me. "I've heard. I also heard you flaunted another man in front of him, one who has been in prison, no less." She scoffs, and it's so loud a piece of her hair flies up.

"I didn't flaunt him. August is a great man, whether or not he's been in prison."

"So it's true. You *are* seeing that boy." She shakes her head. "I expected this from Rhianna, but you, Rylee? Why you? Did I not give you enough love, that you have to go in search of it in all the wrong places? Because that boy is never going anywhere, and as a consequence, *you* will never go anywhere, as *you* will have his name attached to *you*."

"Is that all you care about?" I ask, clearly confused by her statement. "Status and power?"

"We live in a world where that matters. You know this. You work on accounts for rich, powerful people."

"August is an amazing man, not a boy, and I like him very much. He treats me better than Anderson ever did in all the years we were together. He makes me happy. Do you care about my happiness, Mother?"

She waves me off. "Don't try to act like you're hard done by. I care for your happiness. That's been my goal all of your life. I want what's best for you, and pressing charges on Anderson is *not* what's best."

"I'm doing it. He physically abused me all throughout our relationship. Manipulated me. Then he tried to…" I shake my head. "God knows what he wanted to do. But I can tell you… none of it was pleasant, and I'm glad I got away. But if I didn't, you wouldn't be sitting here, Mother. You would be visiting me in jail or the hospital. Would you have preferred those outcomes instead?"

"You know I wouldn't," she sneers, her hands playing with her skirt. I watch her nervous tick and shake my head.

"You'll have to deal with it because Anderson deserves what he gets. He's gotten away with things for way too long to be let off again."

"You'll ruin everything," she whispers.

"No, Anderson did that all by himself," I reply while smiling at her.

"I agreed to a family dinner this weekend, and you're invited," I tell August as I enter his shed later that evening. I should've gone home, but somehow, I found my way back here. He looks up, covered in sawdust, and shakes his head.

"I'll pass," he replies, going back to what he was doing.

I enjoy watching him work, the way his muscles flex when he works and the concentration that's etched on his face.

I enjoy a lot about August Trouble.

"Please… I already told them you're coming."

"We aren't a couple, rich girl. We are just two people who enjoy each other's company and who fuck."

"I want more than a fuck."

"Then you are shopping in the wrong store."

"But am I?" I ask, sashaying over to him. "Because you seem to be enjoying me as much as I am enjoying you."

He lifts his hand, his muscles clenching when he does, and he runs it through his hair and shakes his head.

"Mistake number one, thinking that." He turns and prowls to the power switch, shutting everything off. "Now, unless you're here to fuck, I think it's best you leave."

"You don't want me to stay?" I ask, confused, and now a little hurt.

"No, you should leave."

I'm taken aback by his words. He doesn't look my way as I step out of the shed or even come out front when I walk out there to get in the car. I drive home, wondering what the fuck is wrong with him. And how we went from okay, to broken, to fucked in two-point-one seconds.

"Ry." My door opens, and Rhianna sits next to me in the passenger seat. "You okay?"

"Mom came to see me today," I tell her. "She told me not to press charges against Anderson."

Rhianna grinds her teeth at my words.

I don't tell her about August because, honestly, I don't even know what's going on.

"Of course she did. That would ruin her squeaky-clean reputation." She leans over, placing her hand on my leg. "But you have to do it. You know that, right?" The same eyes as mine are staring back at me. "I met that girl he knocked up. She's young, only a little older than Beckham. Think of all the ways he would manipulate her." I cringe at her words. "You know I'm right because he did it to you."

"I'm going to do it," I state.

"Good. So, how is August, and why are you sitting in your car?"

"He told me to leave."

"Awww, yes, those feelings have hit him hard." She laughs. "I saw it play out on his face. It was like watching a musical with no music."

"He doesn't want me the same way I want him."

"Yes, he does, but that man is confused as hell." She gets out of the car and gestures for me to as well. Following her inside, she throws her arm around my shoulders, kicking the door shut once we're inside. "I'm pretty sure he loves you, but maybe just give him time. He hasn't had anyone care for him all of his life. His mother is a drunk, his father never existed in his life, and his so-called friends used him."

"How do you know all this?"

"Noah," she says, giving me her explanation. "Noah likes him, says he's a good man. It's the reason he fought so hard to get him out of that place."

"But what is good anymore?" I say with a heavy sigh. "I never thought Anderson was evil, and I was so terribly wrong there."

The door to our apartment is kicked open and Beckham's gaze lands on me, his eyes red as he makes his way over to me.

When did he become a man?

"You're okay?" he asks while scanning me up and down.

"I'm fine." I reach out, pulling him in for a hug.

"Hey, how come she's the favorite? You know we're twins, right?" Rhianna jokes.

I pull back, smiling at Beckham. "Who told you?"

"I heard Mom and Dad arguing. Dad was going off."

"What about?" Rhianna asks.

"Mom said she told you not to press charges, and Dad said she was a silly idiot for telling you that, and if you didn't do it, he'll do it for you."

"Go, Dad," Rhianna says. "I don't think he's ever gone against what she wants."

"Rylee, you are the golden child to him," Beckham says.

"Yeah, don't we all know it," Rhianna says with an eye roll, then she nudges me. "Ice cream and donuts?"

Beckham takes off his baseball hat and nods.

How can anyone say no to that combination?

CHAPTER 24

August

Noah tells me how Rylee is, and she called me last week. I haven't seen her since the night I told her to leave.

What does she expect from me? I'm not a man who can give her what she wants. I have nothing to give. It's not who I am.

"August." I hear my name being called as I am finishing up the third coat of varnish on the final of the ordered desks. Turning off the music, I head around to the front of the house.

My mother is standing on my porch, peeking in the window through the open blinds.

"What are you doing here, Carina?"

She turns fast and offers me a guilty smile.

Yes, guilty.

"You've done this place up nice."

"Are you drunk?"

Her eyes go wide at the accusation. "No."

"High, then?"

"No. Look, August... I know you hate me." I harumph at her words as she walks down the steps to where I'm currently standing. "But I've come here as your mother."

"Is that what you're calling yourself these days?" I scrub my hand through my hair. "Could have fooled me."

"August, will you shut up and listen?"

"What do you want? Money?" I ask, reaching into my pocket and pulling out a twenty-dollar bill, then throwing it on the ground at her feet. Her eyes follow it before she looks back at me. "That's all I have. Take it and leave."

"That girl of yours... her boyfriend. He's been coming by to see Josh, and your name has left their lips a few times."

I'm shocked. "Why are you telling me this?"

"You two pissed him off, and she's pressed charges."

I know all this, Noah's told me, but I have no idea what her angle is right now. "And?"

"He wants payback." She rushes the words out, but her cheeks redden, then she drops her head probably in shame. But then again, who really knows with this woman and what she's capable of. Feelings are not something I have felt or even noticed from her.

"Of course he does, poor little rich boy," I say with a head shake. "What's Josh got to do with it?"

"Josh went to him. That little secret I am guessing you're keeping from your new girl? Well, they both know now."

I grind my teeth.

"Maybe you should tell her before he does." She glances at the house. "Can I come inside? I haven't seen it for so long."

Even though I think twice about it, I step aside so she can enter. I watch as she steps in, her eyes taking in everything. She steps into the kitchen, her hand running along the counter before she turns back to me. "No one says no to Josh, and you've done it multiple times. I'm worried for you."

"Now you choose to worry?" I ask her incredulously. "You've got to be fucking with me, right?"

"No, no, I'm not. Josh... he's changed since you went in. He had to get stronger. Do things himself. He lost most of his men after you went inside."

"I don't care."

"He wants you dead. He thinks that'll fix his problems. They see you not working for him again and realize his hold on you wasn't as strong as he said when you went away."

"His hold on me was always weak. I did it purely for the money. I did it all for the money because my own mother didn't bother to fucking feed me."

Her hands go to her chest, and she shakes her head. "I'm going to get help. Rehab. I'm leaving straight after this. I need it."

"You need more than rehab," I tell her. "But that's a start, I suppose. Maybe you can be a better mother to Paige. But me... I'll always know who you are. And believe me, the forgiveness train has well and truly left the station."

My mother's once dark, vibrant hair has faded, and her eyes are sunken into her skull. She appears older than she really is, and beneath all that, I still think she's beautiful.

"I love you, August. I had too many demons that I loved more." Her hand drops from the counter, and she moves to touch my shoulder. "I'm sorry I was an awful mother to you. I know you don't believe me right now, but I really am." She leans up, kisses my cheek, and I watch as she briskly strolls out the door.

"The Harleys are having a small birthday party for me tonight, and I was hoping you would come." Paige sits next to me, holding out a plate full of donuts, so I take one and bite into the delicious treat. "I'm sure Rylee would love to see you." She nudges my shoulder.

"What do you want for your birthday?"

"For you to come to my party. Please. It's nice of them to do this. Dad said you should come, too."

"Your father is going?"

"Yes. He said to make sure I invite you."

I've seen her father a few times over the last week, and I fucking hate it. Going into that police station gives me nothing but concern, but it's over with now. Thank fuck.

Just as I am about to tell her no, I hear a knock on my door. Paige now knows not to answer, so I stand and open the door to Glenn, who's standing there.

"You aren't dressed?"

No, I'm not. I'm still in my work clothes. I was hoping to shower and pass the fuck out after Paige left.

Glenn checks his watch. "We have to leave in ten minutes. Did Paige not tell you?"

"I was just telling him," she says innocently. "He's going to head up and get ready now." She reaches out and hugs my arm. "Aren't you?"

"Paige, don't pressure your brother into things he doesn't want to do," Glenn states.

"I'm not. He asked me what I want for my birthday, so I told him."

Glenn sighs at Paige's words and shakes his head. "You don't have to come if you don't want to."

"I'll be ten minutes." I turn and head straight for the shower, wash, dry, and get into some clean clothes. When I come back down, Paige has changed into a dress and is standing at the door with Glenn.

"Yay! I'm so excited. Beckham has planned it all."

Glenn shakes his head. "Lucky for you, that boy adores you." Glenn walks out and I follow.

We all slide into the car, and Paige stays glued to her phone for the whole ride.

"You nervous?" Glenn asks.

"Should I be?" I ask.

"I don't know. Have you been to the Harleys before?"

"No," I answer.

"Mrs. Harley is quite different... just a word of warning."

Paige laughs from the back seat. "She isn't all *that* bad. She just has high expectations..." She pauses. "Especially for Rylee more than anyone else." Paige almost whispers the words.

"Yes, Rylee's always been the *special child*. She molded everything around her," Glenn declares. "She's taking over the family business. Clever girl, that one."

"We're here." Paige gets out before the car even comes to a full stop.

"If you need to leave, let me know. I'm good at escaping these things," Glenn offers while getting out and following his daughter.

I've seen the house before, but tonight for some reason, it seems bigger. The door opens, and Beckham greets us. He catches Paige as she flies into his arms, and I can hear her giggles as the door is pushed open wider. Rylee is standing there with a smile on her face until she glances my way.

Glenn taps me on the back as I stay at the foot of the stairs. "Good luck," he whispers before stepping to his daughter. Paige ends up pulling herself away from Beckham so he can shake Glenn's hand.

Rylee steps out the door and marches down the two steps to me. "You're here..." she trails off.

I slide my hands into my pockets. "It's her birthday."

Rylee checks back over her shoulder. "I'm aware. It's why I'm here."

"Good to know."

"Are you avoiding me?"

There are three sets of eyes watching us when I look past her.

"We should go in. They're waiting." Rylee peeks back over her shoulder.

"Can you give us a minute?"

Beckham nods then ushers Paige and Glenn inside the house, closing the door behind him. When Rylee turns back to me, her eyes, as dark as the night sky, pin me in place. "You've been avoiding me."

"No, I've been working."

"Working at avoiding… yeah, I get it. You don't want the same things I want. But I'd still like you in my life."

"I'm here right now… in your life," I tell her.

"You're here for Paige, which I'm glad for. But I have a feeling you didn't come willingly."

Opening my mouth to reply, the front door opens again. We both turn to an older version of Rylee. Her eyes squint as she glares at me, then gives the same glare to Rylee. "It's time you come inside. She's about to open presents."

"Yes, Mother," Rylee says.

Her mother turns her nose up and stands there holding the door open.

"This isn't finished. You aren't the villain in my story, August. So stop pretending you need to be." Rylee makes her way up the steps and waits for me to join her.

"Is your friend coming?" her mother asks with raised eyebrows.

"Yes, he is," Rylee says with a bite in her words.

With a sigh, I walk up the steps until I'm next to her and nod at Rylee's mother. "Thank you for inviting me, Mrs. Harley."

She turns her nose up and her eyes wander up and down my body. "I didn't, but it seems you're here anyway."

Rylee gasps next to me.

"I can leave if it's an imposition that I'm here."

"Nonsense. August, isn't it?" A man steps next to Rylee's mother. "Poppy doesn't do well with strangers. I'm Fred Harley, and it's great to have you here." He offers his hand, and I shake it. Rylee doesn't leave my side as Paige and Glenn come to check where I am.

"Go inside. Let's have a drink and talk," Rylee's mother, who I now know as Poppy, says.

"Your sister not here yet?" her father asks Rylee.

"No. She told me she and Noah are running late." They move in the direction of what I can only describe as a sitting room.

When I glance back at Poppy, her mouth is in a thin line, and I'm sure if she could bare her teeth to me, she would. She leans in close and says, "I know who you really are, August. Stay away from my daughter. It's a threat, not a warning," she bites out as she steps past me and heads off to where everyone is waiting.

Taking a deep breath, I close my eyes, center myself, and then make my way inside the room.

Why the fuck I agreed to come to this party, I will never know.

CHAPTER 25

Rylee

August's hands stay in his pockets as he stands near the entry of the living room, as close to the door as he can get, so he can make an escape at any minute if he needs to. With quick steps, I walk over to Paige and kiss her cheek, wishing her a happy birthday as I hand over her present. She pulls at the ribbon and paper with enthusiasm until she comes to what's inside.

"We all know about your love for cooking, so it's a two-day course with one of the best chefs in the area," I explain to her.

She screams and jumps into my arms, kissing my cheek. "This is the best present ever! Thank you, Rylee."

Beckham pulls her back down, and she goes on to the next gift.

I walk over to August and nudge his arm with my shoulder. "Want to get a drink?" His head swivels in my direction, his eyes are hard and lips are thinned. It's as if he's protecting his words. "Come on, you need it." I slide my hand down his arm until it falls into his hand, and I grip tight. Pulling him away, I take August into the kitchen.

He skims me up and down, assessing me before his eyes lock on mine. "You look good."

"Thanks to you," I tell him truthfully. With August, I feel safe. He makes me feel things I haven't felt in such a long time. I like that about him. I like that, with him, his hands never touch me out of anger. They only ever pleasure me.

"Did you press charges?"

"Yes, his family..." I shake my head. "You don't want to know about that." I blink a few times and then ask, "When can I see you again?"

"You're seeing me right now."

"You know that's not what I mean."

"There you two are." My mother comes into the room. "You should both come back into the sitting room. We are going to cut the cake soon."

"We will," I reply.

She's hovering.

Way too much.

I watch as she looks at the glass in August's hand, then at me.

"Please don't leave him in my house unattended. You do know what he went to prison for, right?" My mouth drops open at her words, and my eyebrows rise so high I think they are going to fall off my face.

Now, that's a new low even for her.

Incredibly mean.

Actually, vile.

"I'm going to leave." August places his drink carefully on the counter, the one he never even got to taste.

"Yes, I think that's best," my mother agrees.

"Yes, so do I," I say.

My mother smirks. August doesn't appear shocked, he simply nods before turning.

I reach for my purse from the counter and then run to the sitting room announcing, "Mother has kicked August out. So, I have to go. Have a great night, Paige."

"Rylee," my mother screeches.

When I get outside, August's standing there

waiting for me, as if he knew I was coming.

"Where to, rich girl?" he asks, smirking.

"You are so hot and cold," I tell him while unlocking my car. "Get in."

I can't help but smile when I turn to face him. "Paige was happy you came. I know it mustn't have been any kind of fun..." He says nothing but does nod his head. "Do you not like me, August? Because I got the impression you did."

August closes his knuckles and raps them on the handle of the door. "Why do you keep wanting to talk about feelings, Rylee?"

I come to a stop outside an ice cream parlor. "Ice cream helps the soul. Come... I bet you've never tasted some of the flavors they have here. Absolutely the best in this town."

He gets out, closing the door and stepping closer to me. "You can be really annoying." He says it, but I can see he doesn't mean it—his eyes are the window to his soul and they are sparkling right now.

"It's one of my most endearing qualities. And you love it." I wink as he glances at me, and we stroll into the ice cream parlor. Looking at all the flavors, I can't help but watch his face as he becomes confused.

"Bacon ice cream?" he says, and the shock is not lost on me.

"August?" We both look up to the guy wearing a white hat with an apron behind the counter.

Neither one of them speak. They simply stare at each other.

"Hi, I'm Rylee."

"I know who you are, Miss Harley," he replies, then his eyes fall back to August. "I tried to contact you. You just—"

"Let's go," August interrupts, gripping my hand so tight it almost hurts.

"No. We came for ice cream," I say, pulling my hand free. "He'll have the bacon."

"I don't want the bacon ice cream."

"I'll have the popcorn," I say to the stranger who's serving us, who also seems to be annoying August.

"I'd like a chance to talk to you," he says, scooping my ice cream. He hands it to me, then looks at August. "August."

"I'll have the same as her…"

"My name is Sully," the stranger tells me.

"It's nice to meet you."

"I went to school with you, well… I was in August's year."

"Oh, yes, you do look familiar." I turn to August. "You don't talk much anymore?"

"No," August replies quickly.

"I've tried, but he won't have it. I'm surprised to see you two together." Sully raises his eyebrow at us.

"We should eat, so I can go home."

I nod at August's words and move over to a small table where we sit.

"He was your friend?" I ask, peering to where Sully is still standing behind the counter. He keeps glancing in our direction.

"Was. I told you those close to me either use me or leave. It's always one or the other."

"Maybe you haven't let the right person in yet."

"Is that an invitation, rich girl?"

"I've been throwing invitations at you, left, right, and center, that you never take," I say, scooping a spoonful of ice cream. He does the same, places it in his mouth then scrunches up his nose. The bowl is then slid over to me.

"I've taken a few. I seem to remember how you taste and feel."

"Remembering how you feel is a favorite of mine, too." I wink.

"August." We both turn to Sully who's standing there, hat in his hand. "I'd really like to talk. I haven't worked with Josh since you went away."

"I'm busy with my girl, Sully. Fuck off."

Well, well, well, my cheeks flush at his words.

His girl.

Turning to me, Sully says, "I'm sorry, I didn't mean to ruin your night." He shakes his head and walks away.

"He was trying," I say.

"And now we're leaving. You coming back to mine or going to yours?"

"Am I allowed at yours?" I ask, standing. I offer a small wave to Sully as we leave. When we get outside, I slide into the car and August follows.

"Do you know what usually happens to people like me?" he asks, gazing out the window to where his friend, or not friend, is currently standing. "We do bad things. We kill. We end up in prison. People like me don't have a future, rich girl. When will you see that?"

"How would you know? You aren't like most people, August. Stop putting yourself down or in those categories." I drive off, but I can feel him staring at me.

"I'm unsure if you're remarkable or just plain stupid," he finally says.

"I'd go with the first one, thanks," I tell him, smiling as I drive to his house.

"I guess only time will tell."

He pushes me against the wall, his hands finding every curve of my body. We didn't talk again, even as we got out of the car at his house, but the minute the door shut behind me, his hands were all over me. Grabbing me in places I only give him access, roaming my body as if I am the last thing his hands will ever touch.

But he does it with such tenderness and roughness all mixed into one.

When his hands touch me, I become lightheaded, and all my mind thinks about is him.

As his forest-green eyes lock onto mine before his lips devour me, I melt.

It's then I know I'll do almost anything he wants.

I was that girl once.

I don't think I'll be that girl again.

But for some reason, this doesn't feel the same. Anderson had his own issues. Issues that don't involve me, but somehow, I became the center of them.

With August, he's never tried to control me. Instead, he tells me to go away at every turn. The more he pushes me away, though, the more I want to be next to him.

My hands reach out for him with the same need his hands touch me with.

August is different. I haven't experienced a

force like him before.

August monopolizes my thoughts, stealing them as a thief steals jewelry in the night.

And I'll never complain.

The first time I saw August, I remember thinking he was beautiful. Even with all his rough edges.

The second time I saw him, I watched him from afar, hypnotized by the way he moved and talked but never smiled.

His demeanor was soured by the past.

His behavior distorted by everything life had thrown at him.

"Rich girl." August pulls me out of my thoughts of him. He leans back just a little to see if I'm still here, still in this, and when I reach for him again, he has his answer. August lifts me, and I wrap my legs around his waist.

Sex. It might be all he's willing to give, but I am willing to take it.

Sex with August is my favorite thing.

His hands, rough from work, feel good against my naked skin, especially when they drag up and down my body.

"Rich girl," he says as I bite down on his neck.

"I have a name," I tell him, pulling back.

"Yes, you do," he says with a smirk, his hand

reaching between us so he can touch me. His hand slides up my skirt, and he pushes my panties out of the way so his finger can enter me.

"You can say it," I tell him breathlessly. I've only heard him say my name once.

August's fingers stop moving. "Do you want to fuck or have a conversation about your name?"

"Both." I smile, my hands stay around his neck.

"Rich girl," he says with a shake of the head. He places me down and leaves me standing there. I watch, shocked, as he walks away to the kitchen. I pull my shirt off, followed by my skirt as quickly as I can. I'm left in only my heels as I step up behind him. He's in the refrigerator reaching for a drink when I move my hands around him and capture his hard cock through his pants.

"August," I say, making him turn, and when he does, his eyes eat every part of me.

"I'm thirsty," he says with hooded eyes. I retreat from him until my back hits the counter, then I climb on top and lie back, lifting my head and opening my legs.

"I am, too."

He steps closer. At first, I think he's going to drop the bottle, but he uses it instead, letting the coldness run up my leg until it reaches my middle, then he pauses, pulling it away and opening it. I watch him do it all because he's quite simply fascinating.

The liquid spills on my belly, and he watches it flow along my skin before his mouth comes down and starts licking it off me. When he has licked it all up, he moves the bottle and the liquid pours out over my vagina.

Then he doesn't miss a beat, bending down to lick, taste, and play.

Soon, though, the bottle is forgotten, and his hands are on either side of my legs, pushing them as far open as they will go while his mouth works circles on my clit. I start humping his face, my hands find his hair, but he never stops. He drinks me in like I'm the liquid in the water bottle. He takes pleasure in tasting me as if I am his favorite four-course meal. And when he inserts a finger and flicks upward, I'm done for.

My legs eventually go slack, and he pulls away only to wipe at his mouth with the back of his hand.

"I'm not thirsty anymore." I smile at his words. "But now I'm fucking delirious with need," he says, pulling his cock out and using his fist, sliding up and down the shaft as he steps up to me.

He slides in, lifts me up, so our bodies are locked together, and fucks me while his mouth finds mine. I taste myself on his lips, and I don't pull away. How can I? My body is his, and I'm just here to watch and enjoy the show.

And what a fucking show it is.

CHAPTER 26

August

We passed out on my floor in the sitting room. After the first time in the kitchen, she pushed me back and got on her knees to make me hard again. Then we proceeded to fuck in every corner of the downstairs area until we finally landed on the rug in the sitting room, both exhausted. She is tucked into my shoulder, her dark hair fanning out behind her, lips slightly parted as she sleeps peacefully next to me.

She wants things I have never given.

Things no one has ever asked from me before.

And I quite simply don't know how to give them.

What if I do?

What if I become a man who's worse than Anderson ever was or could be?

She moans in her sleep and hooks one of her legs over me. Then, as if she isn't sleeping, her body starts moving until she's basically on top of me. I hold her to me, and when I do, her eyes pop open.

"Morning."

"Good morning indeed," I say as she slides down. I'm already hard—it's a constant around her.

Rylee leans forward and kisses the side of my mouth as her hips start sliding back and forth. I am powerless to stop her, not that I want to. Her hands grip my shoulders hard, and when I look up at her, I can see the mark on her neck from me, from my mouth.

She'll have to cover that.

I let her go at her own pace. This is her show, and who am I to stop her? I feel when she starts to come, her pussy squeezing around my cock, which makes me come as well. She starts moving faster, her hands digging in further as her head tips back. I reach for her tits, cupping and squeezing the nipples. Her hands cover mine as we come down.

"I have to get ready," she says, then proceeds to lie on my chest, her hair fanning over my face. "I have work."

I smack her ass, and she yelps, then giggles.

"Do you see it?" she asks, pulling back carefully once she gets off of me.

"See what?" I ask, sitting up and watching her grab her clothing and start to get dressed. She doesn't answer until her car keys are in her hand and she's walking out the door. Those dark eyes slide over to me, her hair cascading down her back in luscious curls.

"How beautiful we could be together." Rylee winks, and then she's gone.

I don't disagree. I think a life with Rylee would be great. But it's not just her, it's everyone else as well.

My life isn't as easy as she thinks it is, and that's the damn problem.

Dreaming of a life with her is the stupidest thing I could do. Reaching for my bag of groceries, I walk out of the store. In the parking lot, I spot them straight away. Anderson and Josh both turn to face me, Anderson looking down on me, as if I'm scum. To him, I might just be, but to me, he is much, much worse.

"We've been waiting," Josh says, his arms crossed over his chest.

Anderson walks over first, his eyes assessing me. He isn't taller than me, he comes to my hairline, and he definitely isn't stronger than me. He may have been the high school football star, but since then, all he's done is party and fuck, and it shows on his body.

I turn to go in the opposite direction when Anderson steps in my way, his eyes flick to my bag and then he reaches for it, pulling out a bottle of cream that Paige requested to make some cakes.

He throws it on the ground, and my eyes follow it as the white substance leaks out in a pattern all over the asphalt.

"I know what you did, you scum," Anderson says, leaning in.

"How am I going to spread that over Rylee's body if it's now on the ground?" I reply. "She likes it when I fuck and taste every part of her."

These words have the desired effect. It makes Anderson's hands bunch into tight fists, and he attempts to swing at me. I drop, seeing his fist coming, then move out of the way. He growls and steps up to me again, and Josh, who is now behind me, kicks at the back of my legs. Only one bends, but it gives me enough leeway to turn and punch him straight in his gut, making him fall to the ground, his breath now gone.

Turning back to Anderson, he smirks and goes to step up to me again.

"Piece of shit, that's all you are," he spits.

"Your mother didn't think so." I smirk, and his

eyes turn to slits as he runs at me. I step out of the way, my foot catching his, making him slide to the ground face-first. He screams but gets back up quickly. All the while, Josh is still rolling around, cradling his stomach like a baby.

"Don't you talk about my mother like that, you piece of shit." He runs at me again, and this time, I let him. When his body makes contact with mine, I have to brace myself for the impact. He may have lost some muscle, but he can still run and tackle, obviously.

"Get the fuck up." We both turn to the rent-a-cop standing next to us, his hand on his belt as he evaluates us.

"Fuck off, Larry," Anderson says, his fist cocking back to hit me. I move, getting back on my two feet as Josh does.

"I'll kill you, August. You fuck everything up. Where's your mother?"

So she really did leave.

Holy shit.

"Where is she?" he screams.

"What do you care?" I ask.

Honestly, why the fuck does he care? He used and abused her. There's no reason he should care about her whereabouts right now.

"She's mine," he says with anger, one hand holding onto his stomach.

"No. It seems she isn't."

"She never loved you. Complained about you all your life," he tells me like it might hurt me. As if those words could do more than make me smile. I don't care about the woman, about what she does with her life or anything else for that matter.

"That's great to hear." I pick up my bag of groceries, trying to move away from the shitshow in front of me.

"Fuck off, Larry," Anderson says again to the rent-a-cop.

"No can do, boys. Videos here show what just happened." He points to the cameras overhead. "So unless you want extra charges, you should leave now," Larry says.

I watch him standing ready for them.

Josh's eyes fall to me, and he smiles, but it's more like a grimace before he grabs Anderson by the arm and marches off.

Slowly, I pick up the rest of my things, and Larry bends down to help me.

"I don't know if you remember me…" He holds out his hand for me to shake. I don't. "Well, Sully speaks highly of you. And those two"—he nods to where they're going—"have always been nothing but trouble."

Larry would, at a guess, be my age. His face appears familiar, but it's been too long and all faces became the same to me.

Except hers.

No, hers stands out like the brightest star in a blue sky.

"You know Sully?" I ask.

He scratches the back of his head. "Yeah, he's my boyfriend."

Okay, well, I didn't expect that. At all. Though, I don't remember Sully ever being with girls in school either.

"He tried to visit you when you were locked up, but your mother wouldn't allow it. She controlled who was able to visit you."

I didn't know that.

How the hell could I not have known that?

"Anyway, he's been talking about you." He turns. "I should go. Nice to see you again, August."

I call out to him as he gets to the door. "Tell Sully to stop by."

"He would love that. I'll be sure to pass on the message."

When I arrive home, he's there in an old beat-up car. Sully's leaning against the door, checking his phone until he notices me. "I was on my way to see Larry when he called. Figured I better not blow my chance, so I came straight over now."

I nod. Sully follows behind me as we step off to the door of my house.

"You and Larry..." I ask him as we enter and walk through the house to the kitchen.

He looks around nervously. "Yeah, he's good. Been there for me since I stopped working for Josh, and gave me a place to live." He shrugs. "I owe him a lot."

"Good." I nod, placing the bag on the counter.

"You have blood there." Sully points to his upper lip, and I wipe at mine. "Josh is using Anderson. It's what he does... uses people to get what he wants." He pauses. "And I've heard he wants you gone since you won't go back to working for him."

"Josh has to realize he can't get everything he wants."

"Yes, but try telling him that." He takes a seat. "Are you doing good? How are you?"

"Why do you care?"

"Your name is on a lot of people's lips, not just because of who you are, but because you're with the Harley girl. And not the sister, but the golden child." I shake my head. "So as your friend, who hasn't seen you in years, I want to know... how are you?"

"My friend?" I ask.

"Yes, of course, I'm your friend. I asked Noah if

I could pick you up the day you were released, but he said it was best he did it to get you settled."

"He was right."

"I worry for you," Sully says. "You've always been by yourself, August, so I know you can survive. But sometimes you need a team, people who have your back."

"And you're one of that team?"

"I love you, man, and not in a romantic way. That's reserved for Larry." He chuckles and so do I. "You are my best friend, so yes... I want to help in any way I can. I'm working a few jobs right now, trying to save up some cash. Do you need work?"

"No."

He nods. "What are you doing?"

I gesture to the table behind him, his eyes find it, and he gets up to touch the surface.

"You've always been gifted. Wow, this is amazing." His hand smooths along the desk.

"Thanks."

We continue to talk, and Sully stays for the afternoon, and he only leaves when Rylee turns up. He makes sure he speaks to her, and she laughs at his words.

And when he's gone, she turns to me and announces, "Josh came to see me today."

CHAPTER
27

Rylee

I knew what the look on his face was going to be before I came, before I opened my mouth. I took away his happiness, but he needed to know.

"What did he want?"

"He couldn't get into the building, so he waited until Shandy and I left for lunch." His forest-green eyes lock onto mine. "What happened to your lip?" I reach to touch it, but he recoils and takes a step back. "He asked if I could give you a message."

"And?"

"He said you need to come visit him tonight at the house." I shrug. "He said you'll know which house he's talking about."

"You should leave," August says.

"August..." I say his name maybe a little more loudly than I wanted and then reach for him.

"Just fucking go, Rylee," he snaps.

My hands ball into fists at my sides. The anger pours from me as I glare at him. "No," I scream. "No! You don't get to dictate everything in my fucking life. My mother's done that enough to last me a lifetime. So, no, you don't get to do it as well. So, August Trouble, stop pushing me away."

"I can push you away if I don't want you," he says, and that hits something inside me.

It hurts.

But when I look in his eyes to see if he's telling the truth, I know he isn't.

He's pushing.

Again.

"Lies. You're good at that, pushing people away, because you've never had love and don't know what to do with it," I tell him. My hand reaches out for him, but he brushes me away.

"You're delusional," he says with a cackle that sounds almost evil.

"No, I'm just a stupid girl in love with an even stupider boy."

He pauses. His eyes go round as do mine. I didn't expect to say that. I didn't plan for that to leave my mouth. Yes, I love him. But I assumed it was a heavy crush, maybe an addiction. I've never felt like I do with August. With Anderson, it was convenient. With August, it's all-consuming.

I go to bed thinking about him.

I wake up thinking about him.

He treats me well, even with all the times he's pushed me away. He only does it because that's all he knows. People push him away, so he reciprocates with his own version.

"I didn't mean that."

"You did," he replies. "And you need to leave. Stay away from Josh. Go."

"No." I step up to him, my hands touch his sides, and he shakes his head while trying to pull me away from him.

"Just go. Go home to your comfortable apartment."

"Why are you being like this? Is your favorite thing to push me away? Do you think if you do it enough, I might not come back?"

His eyes lock on mine. "There will be a time when you don't come back. It's a part of life."

"Not mine. I'm like glue, baby. I'm stuck until the end of time." This time I reach up, so my lips touch his. August doesn't kiss me back at first, until I push my body into his, and he gives in. His lips move, and his hands find their way to the most comfortable place, my hips.

Once, I had hands on me that weren't welcome.

Once, I had words whispered in my ear that weren't invited.

I know now, thanks to August, that I shouldn't accept that life.

Why would I?

He doesn't.

Hell, August doesn't accept anyone.

He pulls back fast, putting some distance between us then he shakes his head. "Stop it! Fuck." One hand lifts and spears through his hair.

Someone bangs loudly on the door behind us. I step aside so he can go to it because I've learned not to go near his door. When he pulls it open, Paige's father is standing on the other side.

"Is Paige here?"

"No, why?" August questions.

"She didn't go to school today. The location is off on her phone, and I can't get a hold of her."

"We'll help. I'll drive, August." I pull my car keys out of my pocket, and August takes them from me. *Guess I'm not driving after all.*

"I'll call if I hear anything," August finally says then closes the door in Glenn's face. He waits a few minutes, then grabs his boots, sliding them on.

"Where should we go first?"

"You're not going anywhere. Stay here and don't fucking answer the door to anyone." He rushes to the door then looks back at me. "Better yet, get your sister to pick you up." Then he pulls on the handle and kicks the door closed behind him. I stare at the door for a moment, shocked, then go out front to my car, where he's climbing into the driver's seat.

"August."

"It's not safe where I'm going. Just. Go. Home." He starts the car and pulls out. I watch as he drives away and run inside to grab my phone.

Rhianna picks up straight away.

"Can you come pick me up?" I know she doesn't have a car, but Noah does.

"Umm... hello to you, too."

The car that was here earlier pulls back into the driveway.

"Can you or not?" I ask.

Sully gets out of the car and makes his way to the front door.

"Yes. I'll be there in ten."

"Thanks." I hang up, grabbing my bag. "August just left."

"Look, I don't know if this is true, but I guess it might be," he rushes the words out.

"What?"

"Josh has Paige. And if I know August, he's figured that out, too. And that's where he's heading."

"Josh," I mutter. "He asked him to go to a house. Which house might that be?"

"It wouldn't be where he's living, probably the other property he used to let August crash at every now and then."

"Where?"

"You can't go there. You don't know them. You aren't in that world. He would've left you behind for a reason. Let August handle it."

"Last time he did something for that man, he was sent away, so... *no, I will not*. Where. Is. It?"

"August will kill me if I tell you. It's not a place for you to go alone."

My sister pulls up in the driveway.

"I'm not alone. So tell me where?"

Rhianna gets out of the car and comes over to us as Sully tells me where. "I should call someone, right?" Sully says. "Do something so he doesn't get in trouble."

"No, don't call anyone just yet," Rhianna says and turns to me. "What's happening?"

"August is about to do something that'll land him back where he doesn't want to go," I say to her.

"Rylee," Sully says as I step off to the car. "Be careful. The August you may walk in on is different from the one you know. He's calm now, but he was never calm before. It's what made him so dangerous." I don't take his words in because August may be a lot of things but a danger to me is not one of them.

I trust that man with my life. I would trust him with anyone I love. That's how much faith I have in him.

"I should call Noah."

"You probably should," I tell her.

I don't know what we might possibly walk in on.

Sully is right. I don't know that part of August's life.

But I have faith he'll get Paige back.

CHAPTER
28

I hear her cry. It's sharp and direct. Pain. That's all I can hear from her screams, and my hands bunch up into fists. The gun in my hand is squeezed tight from the pressure as I push through the old door.

"Paige," I say her name, but all I get back in return are cries. Her cries.

"You came. I knew you would." Josh's voice taunts me. "They all think you're a badass, but what they don't know is you're overprotective of those you care for. Including this cute little thing."

Paige screams again, her cries now even louder as I start moving closer.

"Come out, Josh," I yell.

"You really think I'm that dumb? No, August. I know better than that. I may have gotten you the first time, but I have a feeling you know better now."

I do. Under no circumstances would I be stupid enough to believe that Josh has anyone's better interest at heart than his own.

He's known for doing everything for himself.

Only himself.

No one else matters.

"I really thought by throwing you in prison I wouldn't have to worry about you again, but here you are... causing fucking trouble, yet again," Josh says.

I hear Paige's soft cries.

"If you leave, and I *mean leave*, August, I will let her go."

He's lying.

Josh is a liar.

"We both know you're lying. Do you really think I am eighteen again and dumb enough to believe your lies?"

The floor creaks in the old house and Josh comes through a broken door, but in front of him he's holding my sister, whose eyes are bright red from crying.

"No. Seems you're playing on the other side of the tracks lately. We aren't good enough for you anymore. No, you're playing with the rich kids now. Don't think we haven't heard you're with that pretty little brunette."

My back straightens at the mention of Rylee.

"What I would do to her. You see, I don't particularly like them this young." Josh pulls on Paige, making her whimper. "I prefer them older, more Rylee's age, a bit more seasoned but still young enough to break, so they heal faster, and I can play all over again."

Josh is known for beating up his lovers, most of them end up in the hospital, and none report him. He scares them way too much for them to ever say anything.

"I'm going to kill you tonight. You know that, right?"

"You make threats when I have access to something you want?" Josh's other hand holds a small pocket knife, and he brings it to Paige's arm. She stays still, breathing in and holding her breath before he starts to apply pressure. I see blood start to well around the point where the blade pierces her skin.

"I learned that if you cut it this way, and deep enough, you die." He starts slicing into her arm. "How long do you think she has before she blacks out?"

The gun in my hand shakes, but there isn't anything I can do. He has Paige directly in front of him. She looks at me with sad eyes and I know she realizes this as well.

"Have you ever seen a loved one die, watched the light fall from their eyes?"

I don't answer him. Instead, I take one step closer.

"I watched my mother die this way. She slit her own wrists in front of me, and I watched. It's a fascinating thing to see life draining away. To know the second life leaves her body, and knowing full well she isn't coming back." He pauses. "Fascinating."

"You are fucked up."

"We know this. You are, too. Just in a different way, though, right?" He smirks. "I heard you like to play, especially with that rich girl."

He has no idea what he is talking about.

Paige's eyes close, and I can see she's becoming tired. A small pool of blood is spreading on the floor beneath her, and there's fuck all I can do about it.

"Paige." I say her name, and she glances up at me and offers me the saddest of smiles. "Drop." She does as I say but doesn't get far as Josh holds her firmly in place, but it's enough that I raise the gun and shoot anyway.

The bullet pierces his shoulder, and he ricochets backward. He lets her go, and they both fall to the floor. I reach out, pulling Paige away from him, and quickly remove my shirt and wrap it around her wrist to slow the blood loss. "You'll be okay. It'll be okay," I tell her.

Paige nods and turns her head back to Josh, who's slowly sitting up.

I stand and rush over to him with my gun raised.

"Don't you want to know more about Rylee? I know things—" Before he can say another word, I shoot him straight in the head.

I don't need to know any more words.

"August."

I walk back to Paige and kneel next to her as I pull out my phone. I call an ambulance and sit with her as we wait.

"I didn't know. I'm sorry."

I brush her hair away. "You don't have to apologize." She trembles in my arms.

As I hear the siren in the distance, the door to the old house opens and in steps Rylee, her face stricken with fear. She hurries over and drops down, inspecting her.

"What can I do?" she asks.

"Nothing. An ambulance is on its way."

She nods, her eyes roaming me, and I know she sees the damage I've done, the blood splatters that cover my body—none of it mine—a mixture of both Josh's and Paige's.

"Josh..." she says as her eyes fall to where he's lying in a pool of dark red blood. She sucks in a heavy breath as the ambulance and police arrive. I lift Paige and hand her over to the EMTs, so they don't walk any farther in and see Josh. Even though I know where this is heading—me, back in prison, away from her.

Dark eyes, so dark they match my soul, stare back at me.

"I have to go and never come back."

Rylee's eyes go wide, and I resist the urge to take her into my arms and tell her everything will be all right and that she is *it* for me.

She's made me breathe again.

She made me see again.

And most of all, she's made me love.

CHAPTER 29

Rylee

His hand brushes my face. Oh, how beautiful this man is. One of the guys makes a noise, and August checks behind him, his beautiful forest-green eyes leaving me.

I reach for him, touching his face, and he turns back to me.

I need to see him.

I want him to see me.

We are inevitable.

August is, and always will be, my beautiful poison.

With one look, one glance, the poison manifests, spreads through your system and takes hold. And I'm a slave to it.

"Don't go."

"It never would've worked anyway, rich girl. You and me, we are on two different planets."

"No," I cry, reaching for him.

August steps back, so I can no longer touch him. He once told me my touch eases all his pain. That it makes him feel whole again.

His touch does that to me and more.

We never should have been, yet we are.

August's name is called, and he shakes his head. He won't let me touch him again. I just want him to know I'm here, that whatever it is, we can do it together.

August's eyes lock onto mine.

"You are everything and more to me. You know that, right?" His hand twitches at his side, and I know he wants to touch me, but he resists.

"Then stay," I cry.

He shakes his head. "I'm not a good man, rich girl, you know this. I tried, and I failed. I wasn't made that way."

The tears fall faster. "You are. You are the best of men. Better than any man I know." I hear a door open behind me. His eyes leave mine, and when he looks away, I reach for his face and pull it back to me. "Stay with me. Don't leave me." His eyes close at my touch, but he's fast, gripping my hand and pulling it away from his face.

"You'll fall in love, have babies, and live a good life," he says. "But none of those things can ever happen with me."

A hand touches my back, and I know who it is straight away.

"Go with your sister. Go back to your life, rich girl."

"You are my life." I cry harder. Tears are falling so fast from my eyes. I can feel the wetness building on my shirt.

"No, I was merely a moment in time. Passing by like a night star. We both knew it could never work. That *we* can't ever work. We are from two different sides of the tracks. And no matter how hard I try, I can never make it over to your side."

I step back at his words, and Rhianna grips me from behind.

"It's time to go. We have to go," Rhianna says with urgency.

"You can still leave. You can go," I say to him.

August looks down at his clothes. Blood has soaked into them. "No, I can't."

"Ry, we have to go," Rhianna says from behind me.

I reach for him fast enough that he can't stop me, my lips touch his, and he doesn't pull back.

Kissing August is like asking for air but struggling to accept it. Because you know if you do, you may never have that feeling again, but if you don't, you may just die.

He is by far the best kisser I have had, and his lips are the last I ever want to touch mine.

I feel Rhianna's hands leave my shoulders as I push myself up and onto August. My body covering his as I try to climb him. I want to be as close as humanly possible.

He has to know.

He has to know we are meant to be together.

Nothing can get in our way.

Nothing.

My lips feel bruised with how hard I kiss him, and he kisses me back with the same ferocity.

As if he knows, just knows, that this is it.

This is our last kiss.

The sirens are closer, and tears run down my cheeks, but I'm unable to pull away.

I can't.

I need to.

This is it.

I have to accept it.

"Ry, we need to leave. *Now!*" Rhianna urges.

I pull away and reach up to touch his lips, my fingers brushing them one last time.

"I had to."

I nod. It's all I can do. What other words can I say? What's done is done. Nothing I can do will change the fact or change what he's done.

"Now go," he says, then screams, "*Go.*"

Rhianna pulls me back, and we run out the door.

I turn back to take one last look at him. August watches me, as he always does, and this time I know, it's goodbye.

My heart shatters in my chest.

How will I survive?

Survive without him.

When he finally made me live again.

OTHER BOOKS BY
T.L. SMITH

Kandiland

Pure Punishment (Standalone)

Antagonize Me (Standalone)

Degrade (Flawed #1)

Twisted (Flawed #2)

Black (Black #1)

Red (Black #2)

White (Black #3)

Green (Black #4)

Distrust (Smirnov Bratva #1) FREE

Disbelief (Smirnov Bratva #2)

Defiance (Smirnov Bratva #3)

Dismissed (Smirnov Bratva #4)

Lovesick (Standalone)

Lotus (Standalone)

Savage Collision (A Savage Love Duet book 1)

Savage Reckoning (A Savage Love Duet book 2)

OTHER BOOKS BY
T.L. SMITH

Buried in Lies

Distorted Love (Dark Intentions Duet 1)

Sinister Love (Dark Intentions Duet 2)

Cavalier (Crimson Elite #1)

Anguished (Crimson Elite #2)

Conceited (Crimson Elite #3)

Insolent (Crimson Elite #4)

Playette

Love Drunk

Hate Sober

Heartbreak Me (Duet #1)

Heartbreak You (Duet #2)

My Beautiful Poison (Wicked Poison #1)

My Wicked Heart (Wicked Poison #2)

Find all of her books on
www.tlsmithauthor.com